THE PALACE BUZZ

D1565292

BY

LINDA LEE SCHELL

Best wishes!

Linda Schell 2016

A GRACIE BOOK   VOLUME TWO

Linda Lee Schell

A GRACIE BOOK

VOLUME TWO

THE PALACE BUZZ

BY

LINDA LEE SCHELL

ALL RIGHTS RESERVED

COPYRIGHT © 2014

FIRST EDITION 2014

PUBLISHED BY

A KINDER WORLD PUBLISHING HOUSE

https://www.facebook.com/AGracieBook

ISBN-13: 978-1495265570

ISBN-10: 1495265579

MESSAGE FROM THE AUTHOR

COMBINING CHILDHOOD INNOCENCE WITH HISTORICAL VERISIMILITUDE AND A DASH OF MAGICAL FANTASY--THAT WAS THE IMPULSE BEHIND MY WRITING THE GRACIE SERIES.

MY HOPE IS TO EXPAND THE IMAGINATIONS OF CHILDREN WHILE SIMULTANEOUSLY EXPOSING THEM TO A VARIETY OF CULTURES AND HISTORIES.

DESCRIPTION

Here she goes again!

Gracie, a dwarf kangaroo from the thirty-sixth universe, is skipping across the cosmos to her dream destination: St. Petersburg, Russia. She's traveling with Gibson, a Maine coon cat whose life she saved when he was unceremoniously dumped in front of a Pennsylvania corn field.

Expectations and reality quickly collide. What she expected to find was a city of wintery white nights, a city dotted with a hundred islands linked by dozens of imposing bridges, all book-ended by majestic sculptures cast in bronze.

She expected to feast her eyes on historic buildings splashed with pink, yellow and blue pastels.

Instead, she finds herself back in the 18th century, in Russia's Imperial Golden Age. *This is not the city I expected*, she laments as she stands bewildered near the entrance to the city's center of activity, the perpetually busy post office.

Then, when Empress Catherine arrives in her royal carriage and points a bejeweled finger at the ever-so-handsome Gibson, and declares: *I want that cat*...the fun begins.

GRACIE'S DEFINITIONS

FOR

AN EASY READING ADVENTURE

ASSUAGE Alleviate, Lessen, Soften, Diminish

ASTUTE Shrewd, Smart, Wise, Clever

BLARNEY Flattery, Smooth talk

BOYAR A member of higher Russian nobility, ranking below a prince, between the 12th and early 18th centuries

CACOPHONY Loud sounds that are irritating and out of tune

CAMISOLE Woman's sleeveless undergarment, Often fancy

CHIDED Gently scold, Express disapproval

CITADEL Fortress, Refuge

COMMODIOUS Roomy, Spacious, Big

CONSORT Companion, Partner,

CONVOY Group, Procession, Line

COPIOUS Abundant, Plentiful, Bountiful

DECOLLETAGE A low-cut neckline on a woman's dress

DIDEROT, DENIS French philosopher, art critic, and writer, Best known for serving as co-founder, chief editor, and contributor to the _Encyclopédie_ along with Jean le Rond d'Alembert

DISCOURSE Conversation, Serious discussion

DUMBWAITER A small elevator used for moving food and tableware from one floor to another

EARMARK To select something to be used for a particular purpose, Assign, Put to one side, Tag, Save

EQUILIBRIUM Balance, Stability

FAMISHED Hungry, Starving

FISSURE A long, narrow opening, A crack, The process of splitting

FREDERICK OF PRUSSIA King of Prussia, Brilliant military campaigner

GRIGORY ORLOV Counselor to Catherine during her reign, and sympathetic to the question of improving the condition of the serfs and their partial emancipation. Came from a noble family

IMPERCEPTIBLY Unnoticeably, Barely, Undetectably

IMPOSING Impressive, Striking, Commanding

MANIC Overexcited, Hyper, Agitated, Frenzied

MATIUSHKA Russian name for mother

MAZE Network, Web, Tangle, Confusion, Muddle

MELLIFLUOUS Smooth

MENDACITY Dishonesty, Fabrication, Falsehood

NAÏVE Inexperienced, Green, Immature

NATTERING Chatter, Blather, Nonsense

NEVESKY PROSPEKT St. Petersburg's most famous street, Renowned for fine architecture and famous residents

ORB Globe, Sphere

PALPABLE Intense, Obvious, Easily observed

PANNIER DRESS A dress that rests on a wire frame. Framework to widen a skirt at each side of the hips, Worn in the 18th century

PAPRIKA A deep orange-red color like that of paprika, A red powder that is made from sweet peppers and used as a spice for food

PAROXYSM Outburst; Fit, Convulsion

PAROXYSM Outburst; Fit, Convulsion

PAUCITY An inadequacy or lack of something, Scarcity

PERIMETER Border, Edge, Outer limits, Outside

PERUKE Man's wig, popular from the 17th to the 19th century

PREAMBLE Introduction, Opening, Something that introduces what follows

PRINCESS DASHKOVA Was the closest female friend of Empress, Catherine the Great, and was a major figure of the Russian Enlightenment. Became one of the leaders of the party that attached itself to Catherine.

PROCLIVITY Liking, Inclination, Tendency

REBUKE To criticize, To reprimand

RESONANT Echoing, Ringing, Significant, Meaningful

RETINUE Entourage, Followers, Attendants

RETAINER A person or thing that retains, Servant who has served a family for many years

REVERIE Daydream, Dream, State of pleasant thoughts
SNIGGER To snicker, Sneer, Giggle

SOVEREIGN Having authority over a geographic area, Having authority over a territory

SPUTNIK Artificial earth orbiting satellite. The first one was launched by the former Soviet Union starting in 1957

TABLEAU Representation, Sometimes means "picture"

TETE-A-TETE   Conversation, One-to-one, Heart-to-heart, Discussion

VELLUM   High quality parchment made from calfskin, Manuscript written on vellum

VOLTAIRE Francois-Marie Arouet, known as Voltaire, A French Enlightenment writer, historian and philosopher, and famous for his wit

Ambassador's (Jordan) Staircase, photo courtesy of saint-petersburg.com

CHAPTER ONE

A space bus zips across the Milky Way.

Inside the capsule--actually a Time Warp Tube--Gracie and Gibson sleep. She is a 'roo, the tiniest of an ancient species of kangaroo-like creatures, hailing from a world just south of the Never-Ending Rainbow in what is quite possibly the oldest and grandest of all the universes.

He is a Maine Coon cat from Pennsylvania.

The pair is on their way to St. Petersburg, Russia, on the planet Earth, having begun their journey in the thirty-sixth universe, a place so far away that the distance is nearly inexpressible: hundreds of thousands of quintillion light-years perhaps.

Safe inside the speeding bullet, Gracie reached down into her pouch and patted the purse holding her Get Well, Stay Well Stuff, the sparkling flakes that 'roos in Gracie's universe rely on for health, well-being, and sometimes safety. Knowing the purse was there gave Gracie a comforting sense of security.

Gibson stiffened and stretched his legs, his paws fanning open to an impressive width.

"I can't wait to get back to earth," he declared eagerly. "I'm getting more excited by the minute."

"Me too," Gracie replied. "We both deserve a vacation after everything that has happened. On the Heinselman farm, you were exhausted from all the mousing you had to do, and I was getting frazzled worrying about how to get back to the thirty-sixth universe to refuel, although my being marooned in Pennsylvania did turn out to be a great adventure. And don't forget, we would have missed a great friendship if the Time Warp Tube had taken me straight to St. Petersburg."

"Maybe some things are just meant to be," Gibson acknowledged. "If nothing else, though, I hope this vacation puts an end to my visions of parallel universes. You have no idea how disturbing they can be."

Before Gracie could reply, there was a thunderous bang, followed immediately by a loud boom. Sirens screeched and screamed, bells clanged and bonged. The noise hurt their ears and befuddled their thoughts. The tube careened to the left, then bounced several times, sending everything in the cabin that wasn't tied down flying through the air. The tube began a downward spiral, pushing Gracie and Gibson to the rear of the capsule.

For the next few seconds, all Gracie's hopes, dreams, and memories raced through her mind. Gracie's life in the thirty-sixth universe was one of supreme privilege. In her idyllic world, 'roos hopped along lanes festooned with pink and red rose petals as they went about their daily errands to places such as the Citadel of Contentment, the Hall of Knowledge and Wonderment, and the Establishment of Abundant Supplies.

Since Gracie's life was devoid of need and strife, she was blessed with the opportunity to pursue any interest or fancy she desired. Because she loved beauty above all else-- yet craved exotic adventure--her goal was to visit St. Petersburg, Russia. Now, in the din and confusion of the spiraling capsule, Gracie feared she would never set eyes on her city of dreams, a city of museums that resembled a gigantic candy dish of eye-pleasing pastel pink, yellow and blue buildings; a city of one hundred islands, connected by more bridges than any place else on the planet.

And what about the ballet, the opera, the theaters, the rare masterpieces of art, the exotic gardens and restaurants? And oh yes, the *humans*!

Another *bang*, this one far louder than the first. Now the Time Warp Tube picked up speed, and the noise rose to a deafening roar. In the confusion, Gracie's tiny 'roo body pressed against Gibson's nose and mouth. The slight suffocation caused a momentary panic; his thoughts returned to last summer when his former owner unceremoniously dumped his twenty-five pound rump in a ditch on a farm in St. Clair, Pennsylvania.

Gracie had been marooned on the same farm earlier that morning when her Time Warp Tube had deposited her beside the farm's cornfield instead of in the heart of St. Petersburg. After Gibson had been attacked by a pair of rowdy farm dogs, Gracie restored him to health with a few specks of her all-purpose Get Well, Stay Well Stuff, although the flakes proved powerless against the bizarre visions of parallel universes brought on by the dogs' trouncing. Nevertheless, out of the mayhem a beautiful friendship was born.

Boom!

A violent blow shoved the tube farther to the left. Then, abruptly, the vessel lost its will to spin and instead settled into an unexpected glide. Neither cat nor 'roo spoke. The fear of the unknown paralyzed their tongues. In the darkness of the cabin, Gracie and Gibson both wondered if they would ever return to the Heinselman farm and see their adopted mistress, the farmer's daughter, again.

Right now, Gibson desperately wanted nothing more than to take refuge in the sheltering oak tree with Gracie, or sit on the farmer's lap and listen to the radio, or feel the gentle hand of his eight year-old mistress on his back.

As the memories of their summer on the farm accumulated in Gibson's mind, the spacecraft settled into a peaceful descent. Within a minute, all sense of motion ceased. Light returned to the cabin. Gibson and Gracie stared at each other in ecstatic relief. The Time Warp Tube had held together. They were safe.

Their fears now forgotten, replaced by eager expectations, the two travelers danced with joy as the capsule door hissed open. Before them lay their long awaited adventure.

St. Petersburg, at last!

CHAPTER TWO

Gibson walked and Gracie hopped down the Time Warp Tube's metal ramp and found themselves in a narrow cobblestone alleyway. Neither spoke as they gazed about their surroundings. A cacophony of unidentifiable yet vaguely familiar sounds assaulted their senses. Then, to their astonishment, a singular voice cut through the din.

"Gracie! Gracie, dear, it's me, your Aunt Zappa."

Gibson froze when an older-looking Gracie suddenly materialized before his eyes. Gracie hopped up and down in unrestrained delight.

"Auntie Zappa! I can't believe you're here! I've always wanted to meet you and—"

"I know you have, my dear, but unfortunately this has to be a brief visit. Talking depletes my energy, and I risk fading away." She turned to Gibson and said warmly, "Incidentally, I want you to know that all of us think you're a marvelous cat, exceptional, in fact. But I really can't talk about that now. I'm afraid there's something quite serious that the two of you need to know."

"What is it, auntie?"

While Gibson awaited the elderly 'roo's reply, he suddenly realized that he could see right through her to the buildings beyond. *Now that's odd.*

"As you may or may not know, the planet Jupiter's function is to protect space travelers from meteorites. Well, for some reason--we don't know why--Jupiter rolled off course by just a hair and allowed a meteorite no larger than a grain of sand to crash into your Time Warp Tube."

"So that's what caused all the commotion," Gracie said. "It got pretty wild there toward the end, but as far as I can tell, we landed without any problem."

"Gracie, Gibson--you're in St. Petersburg, the land of white winter nights. The problem is ..."

Uh-oh, Gibson thought. Beside him, Gracie held her breath.

"The problem, my dears, is that you have landed in Russia's Imperial Golden Age. It's the seventeen hundreds, earth time, not 1958."

As if on cue, a man and a woman appeared at the end of the alley. As they sauntered by, Gracie and Gibson saw that the man was dressed in white stockings and black shoes with high heels. His lady friend, who was clutching his arm and gazing into his heavily powdered face, was attired in a gaily-colored panniered dress.

"In case you're wondering," Auntie Zappa explained, "the clothes they're wearing are all the rage among the aristocracy. That man's wig is called a peruke."

Gibson's mouth dropped in awe. He envied the cascade of white curls reaching to the man's shoulders. He'd never seen such an abundant mane of hair on a man before.

Gracie, on the other hand, couldn't take her eyes off the woman's dress. She loved the way the sides puffed out at the hips. What Gracie didn't realize was that the dress actually rested on a wire frame, similar to a lampshade.

"Now," Auntie Zappa continued, "if you can ignore these rather peculiar fashions, there are some important matters you need to consider."

"Wait," Gracie interjected. "What's that noise down the street? It sounds like a riot."

Gibson's ears cupped forward as he focused in on the clamor. The ruckus disturbed him, though he didn't know why.

"The sounds you're hearing are made by rare animals. They're considered valuable curiosities. The collection is known as a menagerie."

"What kind of animals?" Gracie and Gibson both asked.

"Monkeys, tigers, leopards, bears, lions, camels, hyenas, peacocks, lynx--far more animals than I can remember. But my point is that you, Gracie, are a curiosity yourself, and the ruling powers here have a passion for collecting curiosities. The rarer the curiosity--and that certainly includes animals--the more status these people accrue--at least in their own eyes. So it's vital that you keep a low profile and not end up in someone's menagerie before we can send a rescue Time Warp Tube. It is expected to arrive in five to seven nights."

Gracie and Gibson groaned.

"Gibson, I'm sure everyone in St. Petersburg has seen a black cat before, though none as handsome as you." Believing Auntie spoke the truth, Gibson glowed with pride.

"Since you're not conspicuous, you can scout for food without being noticed."

Gibson thought this made perfect sense. He felt entirely relaxed around this translucent figure who apparently was Gracie's ancient ancestor. *Go figure.*

"Any suggestions where I should start hunting?" Gibson

asked.

"Yes. Stay right here at the post office," the elderly 'roo advised, pointing up at the stately stone building bordering the alley.

"The *post office*?"

"It's not just a post office. It's a social hub in this part of the city. It doubles as a hotel and a tavern, and there's a ballroom for special events. Tonight you can listen to the brass band. It'll be fun. Gibson, you're clever. Cajole some food from the cook at the post office eatery. I recommend you sample the black caviar and dumplings." Aunt Zappa chuckled at her own suggestion. "And Gracie, I think you would enjoy the cabbage soup."

Gracie frowned skeptically, but respectfully held her tongue.

"Now, I'm afraid I'm running out of energy already," Auntie Zappa declared. Her eyes fluttered as she fought to retain her equilibrium. "At my age, I've got to be careful not to overdo things. It's been a pleasure meeting you both. Good luck and remember: there's danger everywhere here."

"Oh, Auntie Zappa, St. Petersburg is a dream come true. I'm sure it'll be everything we hoped for. How can you say--"

"Gracie, not long ago, Czar Peter the Great ruled this land. In his day, wolves roamed these streets. Just stay safe until we can transport you to the twentieth century. I'll come back and check up on you if I can."

Then, before they could even offer a goodbye, the ancient 'roo faded away into nothingness.

CHAPTER THREE

A horse-drawn carriage creaked along the boulevard. Inside the finely-crafted gold and silver-trimmed coach was a troop of weary royal travelers. The dozing passengers rested on red velvet seats that had been painstakingly adorned with embroidered flowers, sequins and faux diamonds.

The coachman reined the four white horses to a halt. The footman, clad in an emerald green uniform, stepped down from his perch and opened the door. A waterfall of stair-steps cascaded to the ground.

Inside this ornate palace on wheels, an eight-year-old boy cried, "Mama, Mama, look at the beautiful cat over there by the post office!"

"General Orlov," the boy's mother declared to the handsome man beside her, "do my eyes deceive me or is that cat actually dragging a dish of food with its mouth?"

"That is indeed what you see, my Royal Empress."

"Mama, look how big and strong he is!"

The woman nodded in agreement.

"Footman," she commanded, pointing a bejeweled finger at Gibson, "I want that cat." Then, turning to her companion, she asked, "General Orlov, would you please be so kind as to deposit this letter at the post office?"

"With pleasure, your Royal Empress." The general climbed out of the carriage and strode briskly across the street. The footman, meanwhile, paused to watch the huge cat drag the plate over the cobblestones. The footman chuckled.

"Just where do you think you're taking that food, you handsome brute?"

Gibson continued pulling the plate, unaware that he was entertaining the occupants of the carriage.

The servant snatched Gibson with both hands. Surprised, Gibson screeched as he felt himself being lifted into the air. He contorted his furry body in anger. Returning from the post office, General Orlov rushed to assist the footman, who needed an additional pair of hands to subdue the panic-stricken animal.

Gracie sprang into action as soon as she heard Gibson's cries of alarm. She jumped into the carriage as the men clamored aboard with their unwilling cargo. The empress and her consort, Princess Dashkova, shrieked as Gracie hopped over, under, and between their feet.

"Get that rodent out of here!" General Orlov roared.

The young boy scooped Gracie up to his lap. Straining to contain the squirming 'roo, the boy said, "Mama, this doesn't look like an ordinary rodent."

Seeing the young boy clutch Gracie's tiny body, Gibson ceased his squirming and clawing. By subduing his anger, he hoped the adults in the carriage would calm down and be less fearful of Gracie.

The empress's lady-in-waiting peered intently at the little animal.

"My lady, I believe your son is correct. I'm not sure *what* it is, but it doesn't look like any rat *I've* ever seen."

"Hmm," the empress mused. "Paul," she said, "allow me; let me examine this cute . . . curiosity."

"You'd best be careful," Orlov warned. "We don't know what it is."

"Gracie," Gibson advised, "be calm and sit still. We don't want these humans to think we might harm them. We'll figure out a way to get out of here later." Gracie took a deep breath and exhaled. The tension in her body disappeared like water flowing down a drain.

Satisfied that calm had been restored, General Orlov motioned with his arm to the coachman.

"To the palace," he ordered.

The coachman cracked his whip and the carriage lurched into motion. Gibson and Gracie looked imploringly at one another as they both pondered the same question: Now what do we do?

CHAPTER FOUR

As the team of high-strung horses trotted along the dusty street, the ornate carriage swayed on its frame like a child's tug boat in a tub. By now Gracie had crawled above the edge of the empress's décolletage dress. With her head resting on the empress's shoulder, Gracie stretched her legs and tucked her tiny toes inside the neckline of the elegant garment.

Gibson, sandwiched between Princess Dashkova and General Orlov, enjoyed the simultaneous treat of having the back of his ears scratched as well as his ample mane affectionately caressed. The mood in the carriage was peaceful. As the empress--whose name was Catherine--gazed upon her slumbering son, the only audible sound was the lad's childish snorts. Biting her lips while lost in thought, the beautiful Princess Dashkova focused her gaze on the passing buildings, gaily colored in pastel hues of green, yellow, and blue.

Taking note of the calm that had settled over his traveling companions, and certain that young Paul was safely tucked into a world of dreams, General Orlov cleared his throat.

"My Royal Empress," he began hesitantly.

"Yes, Orlov, what is it? Something is weighing on your mind. I hope you're not going to upset me."

"I'm afraid it concerns the Czar, my Royal Empress. While you were gone--"

"Ah, let me guess. The situation has worsened, hasn't it?"

"Considerably."

"How so?"

"Simply put, he's making a mockery out of the palace. His behavior is an embarrassment to the throne. He's a disgrace to Russia." Orlov appealed to the young woman beside him. "Princess Dashkova, please help me find the right words here."

Without hesitation, the princess complied.

"He's a simpleton, your Highness."

"And a nincompoop," added the general.

Feeling a miniscule change in the empress's body tension, Gracie flexed her claws ever so slightly into her host's billowy soft bosom. Gibson's tail lifted, then floated down gently upon the cushioned seat.

"Be specific, general. What has our beloved Czar Peter, grandson of Peter the Great, done this time to agitate you?"

"He's confiscated our Imperial Guards' splendid green uniforms and ordered our soldiers to wear the Prussian blue. He prattles nonstop to the boyars about what a great fellow Frederick of Prussia is."

"Those are foolish words. If he's not careful, the nobles will cut off our heads."

General Orlov lowered his voice as if to share a secret.

"I tell you, I think Czar Peter wants to turn the motherland into Prussia."

"I've no doubt he'd like to, but I still think he lacks the wherewithal to act on his convictions. Luckily for us, his organizational skills are feeble at best."

"I hope you're right," the general sighed, "for all our sakes."

Conversation ceased as the royal carriage turned into the grandest street in all of St. Petersburg: Nevsky Prospekt. Two rows of imposing shade trees splashing red and gold autumn colors lined both sides of the expansive roadway, echoing the glory days of ancient Rome and serving now to remind the weary travelers that they would soon be home.

Taking in the bizarre sight of Gracie resting her head on the Empress Catherine's shoulder, the general smiled broadly and declared, "I don't think our little flat-footed friend here gives two hoots about the Prussians. Look at her. She just wants her mother."

Princess Dashkova nodded in agreement. The general went on to observe, "You see, my Royal Empress, like little Flat Foot holding on to you so tightly, your people, too, want their matiushka. I beg you, on behalf of your people, be their mother. They need their matiushka."

The empress let out a deep breath, "I know they do, general, and like a good matiushka I will never turn my back on those who depend on me."

"And the people know that," Princess Dashkova interjected.

"Yes," the general said, "but they want more than a shoulder to lean on. They want a strong matiushka; they want a leader."

"I ache for my people, Orlov, but I cannot take on such a heavy duty in haste."

"Matiushka, it's not just the princess and I who want you to save Russia. The Imperial Guard stands ready to support you, as well. The entire palace needs your guidance."

As the empress gazed through the window of the carriage, her view was blurred by an unexpected welling of tears. She patted Gracie tenderly and allowed her thoughts to turn inward.

The coachman slowed the horses to a measured trot as they approached the palace. The change in movement roused Gracie from her nap. Gibson placed his front paws on the beveled glass to observe the panorama as the carriage neared what looked to be a pink cotton candy palace sprinkled with thousands of windows trimmed in white sugar icing.

At the palace gate, a handler cajoled a dancing bear with snacks of fish, while a boy playing the flute entertained a tiny gathering.

Beyond the palace, in a tall tower, four monks sprang into action, grappling with massive gnarled ropes that lifted their robed bodies like yo-yos in their effort to get the massive bell swinging.

Bong. Bong. *Bong.*

A resonant peal floated out across the city, announcing to the citizenry that their beloved Empress Catherine and her son had returned safely and were once again in residence at the palace.

CHAPTER FIVE

With heavy hearts and empty stomachs, the imperial travelers climbed the palace stairs, trailed by a long line of baggage-ladened servants. Princes Dashkova hugged Gracie to her breast while Gibson peeked through the unbuttoned front of Orlov's disheveled uniform, his tail bandying left and right through the unfastened bottom of the long green tunic.

With the empress and little Paul leading the procession, the human convoy was forced to jump aside as a blustering peacock, wings flailing, came racing down the staircase as if fleeing for its life. A trio of rats, lurking behind a massive marble column on the landing, paid no mind to either the humans or the giant squawking bird; instead, their noses twitched as they caught the scent of a deliciously foul stench wafting from the Czar's spacious second-floor chambers.

Although alert and curious, Gracie and Gibson could not fully absorb all the grandeur, confusion, and smells of the palace. They were surrounded by a spectacle of ornate ceilings, sparkling chandeliers and oddly shaped candelabras. The palace was a maze of mirrored rooms, some with walls crafted in precious amber, malachite, and jasper. Huge granite and marble columns connected inlaid floors to forty-foot ceilings. Now, as they completed their ascent up the staircase, the royal entourage heard the distant sound of clomping feet coming from the Czar's chambers. Moments later, a squad of Imperial Guardsman shuffled into the hallway landing.

"Squad, halt!" ordered a burly, mustached sergeant. The soldiers froze in place. Their leader executed a well-practiced bow to the empress, then smartly saluted General Orlov.

Noting the flushed faces of the soldiers, the empress inquired, "Sergeant, why are you and your men perspiring so heavily? It's not particularly warm in here."

"We were . . . exercising, your Highness."

"Ah. In your new blue uniforms, I see."

"Yes, my Royal Empress." The sergeant blushed, his red face matching those of his men. "Czar Peter has drilled us in his chamber every day since you departed on your journey. He dismissed us less than a minute ago."

The empress turned and shot a knowing glance toward Orlov and the princess as if to say: *We're already well-acquainted with the Czar's penchant for nonsense.*

Already exasperated and losing patience because of the pitiful state of affairs in the palace, General Orlov turned on his heel and shouted down to a man standing near the bottom of the stairs.

"Malatov! You're the Czar's valet. What is that disgusting smell?"

All eyes on the staircase focused on Sergie Malatov. Fearful that an honest answer might only arouse more ire, the servant hesitated.

"Don't stand there like a fool! Speak!" the empress commanded.

In a nervous voice, the valet explained. "Twice a day, my lady, the Czar drills his hunting dogs, all twenty of them. He makes them run from one end of his chamber to the other. Because he loves his dogs he makes sure they are always well fed and watered, which means that . . . they frequently succumb to nature. I'll make sure the mess is cleaned up as soon as the Czar allows it, which, I have to admit, is not always as prompt as I would like."

"Protect us," General Orlov muttered in disbelief.

Gracie, sensing that the tiny meteorite had knocked her and Gibson into a truly loopy era in Russia's past, began to feel unnerved. Seeking comfort and escape, she slid further down into the princess's dress. Gibson, meanwhile, was having his own misgivings about this zany kingdom. Earlier in the carriage, Gibson had heard General Orlov remark to his companions that they were fortunate to be living in the Age of Reason.

"If people would only follow the precepts of the Age and apply logic they would surely find answers to all their problems," he'd said.

Theories and formulas were all well and good, Gibson thought, *but judging from what I've seen so far here at the palace, there is nothing reasonable about the Imperial Age of Russia. Rather, it seems more like the Age of Mayhem and Confusion.*

The sergeant interrupted Gibson's musings by barking out, "Forward, march!" The soldiers stomped down the stairs, leaving the empress and her companions to make sense of what had just transpired. In silence, servants and sovereign pondered the apparent palace chaos. It was Paul, the empress's son, who spoke first.

"Mama," he said, "I hear strange sounds coming from

papa's chamber."

The noise, which they could all hear now, was a babble of words and a clatter of heels smacking, clacking and whacking the floor of the Czar's chamber. The boy squeezed his mother's hand and grinned broadly as he looked up at her.

"I bet I know who's making all that noise! It's Ivan and papa."

A vision of Ivan---adorable Ivan---crossed the empress's mind, bringing a smile to her lips and sparkle to her eyes. Making no effort to conceal her delight, the empress giggled ever so slightly and agreed with her son.

"I think you're right, my dear. It probably is our Ivan and papa."

Pleased to hear his mother agree with him, the child asked eagerly, "Everyone loves Ivan, don't they, mama?"

Upon hearing this unequivocal declaration of admiration for Ivan, the nearby servants rolled their eyes in disbelief. *They* were unanimous in their collective loathing of Ivan, the palace terror.

Catherine, however, paid them no heed. Noting it was already mid-afternoon and her stomach was growling, she instructed one of the servants to bring copious amounts of food to her quarters. Next, the empress ordered Malatov to accompany Paul to her chambers where the boy could rest while their food was prepared.

The child grasped the valet's hand, and the two of them ascended the stairs to Catherine's apartment. As much as Paul wished to inquire further about his adored friend Ivan, he did not cross his mother; if she wished him gone, he knew better than to linger.

As the valet and well-behaved little boy trooped down the corridor, Catherine said to Princess Dashkova, "Your gracious presence and good cheer bring me much satisfaction. Please share a meal with us."

"With pleasure, my Royal Empress."

"And you as well, General Orlov."

"Of course, my lady." As the middle-aged but still handsome officer bowed, his chin pressed against Gibson's head, causing the cat to take in a quick gasp of air.

Noting the red highlights in Gracie's fur as she was resting contently on Princess Dashkova's breast, an idea sprang to life in Catherine's mind.

"Princess Dashkova, before the day is over, go to my wardrobe and fetch the trunk I retrieved from my parents' home. Select a dress from one of my dolls for our *Paprika* here. You can slit an opening in the seam for her little tail."

"What a splendid idea," the princess declared, happy to be included in the empress's make-believe world. She immediately took her leave and hastened up the stairs in search of the empress's childhood trunk of treasures.

For her part, Gracie was thrilled by the empress's idea. By wearing a regal gown, she would be part of the royal family. Princess Paprika. *Yes*, she thought. *I definitely like it.*

Gibson, meanwhile, was growing increasingly uncomfortable under Orlov's coat. He squirmed, craning his neck for air. Orlov patted him reassuringly on the head.

"It won't be much longer, Pepper," the general whispered into his new friend's ear. "Since her Highness gave her creature a name--Paprika--I've decided to name you Pepper. That is, if the empress and Paul agree."

The general directed his gaze upward toward the gilded ceiling, not wanting to reveal disrespect by showing his true thoughts. Shadows danced along the walls from the lighted candelabras as Orlov envisioned Flat Foot in a billowing silk dress. The general shook his head. No one in the czar's army, from the highest general to the lowest private, would believe that their empress, a lady who played the harp like an angel and who read the writings of the ancient Greeks, would play house with a flat-footed rodent. But the empress was the empress, so . . .

"The rest of you can proceed to my chambers and begin unpacking," Catherine announced to the remaining servants. "And be careful. I don't want anything broken."

Knowing better than to dawdle, the small army of servants sprang into action, lifting the many trunks and suitcases, all bearing the imperial emblem, and set off to complete their assignments.

Alone finally with Orlov, the empress said, "General, before I join you in my chamber with the princess and Paul, I'm going to pay a visit to the czar. I wonder what he's so engrossed in that he's completely unaware that we have returned from our journey."

"As you wish," Orlov replied, his eyes meeting Catherine's. Both knew that whatever intrigue lurked in the Czar's chamber would be a matter for concern. With a flourish, Orlov clicked his heels together, nodded ever so slightly, and walked away.

Catherine took a deep breath to steady her nerves. As she approached the massive birch and walnut door to the Czar's chambers, she wondered what new and no doubt exasperating foolishness she would discover on the other side.

CHAPTER SIX

Catherine knocked. Ever so slowly, the fifteen foot door creaked open. Peering out at her were the blue eyes, long nose, and weathered face of the czar's personal manservant.

"Your Royal Empress," he declared without smiling, "it's good to have you home again."

"I need to see the czar," she declared without preamble. "I realize this may not be a convenient time, but I promise not to disrupt his soldier games for very long.

The frail-looking retainer leaned forward against the door, pushing it open inch by inch until the empress was able to slip into the monarch's luxurious amber and gold apartment. Leaving the servant behind, Catherine strode briskly across the enormous room until she reached a spot maybe five feet directly behind the czar. What she saw dismayed her. While Peter clacked and whacked his high-heeled boots on the inlaid floor, a tiny monkey swayed atop the czar's shoulder. Its pink round face gazed upward in delight at the sparkling chandeliers. From its mouth, filled with razor-sharp teeth, came a steady flow of squeaks, barks, and growls.

"Come along, Ivan, sing with me this time," cajoled the czar. "You can do it. Sing, Ivan, sing!"

The monarch took a deep breath and unleashed a shrill

off-key "Oh . . ." before launching into the lyrics of his own made-up song.

I want to be a Prussian, not a Russian

I want to strut in my cloth of powder blue

Give my green to the blarney Irish; I care not with it what they do

I want to be a Prussian not a Russian

I want to strut in my cloth of powder blue

Give the word to the boyars, for I care not what the nobles think or do

I want to be a Prussian, not a Russian

I want to eat their stringy sauerkraut

I'm rushin' to be Prussian, 'cause Prussian's what I'm about.

"Bravo!" the czar shouted at the conclusion of his little song and dance. "You did well, my little friend, but that's enough for one day." Czar and monkey each patted the other on the head. Peter deposited Ivan on the floor and reached for his violin and bow that lay atop a marble credenza. Hoisting the instrument to his shoulder, he swiveled round on his heel and was about to launch into an improvised ditty when he saw his wife, hands on hips frowning her disapproval at him.

"Catherine. . . !"

The monkey, who was maybe half the size of Gibson, chirped delightedly and ran toward his mistress, extending a tiny hand in greeting.

The empress took Ivan's hand and smiled, "Hello, Ivan." Her spirits lifted as she gazed at the creature, feeding off his friendliness.

Returning her attention to Peter, her pleasure vanished. Before her stood the sovereign of Russia, and the sovereign, her husband, did not want to be a Russian.

"Peter, I demand an explanation! How dare you declare your allegiance to Prussia! After all the sacrifices our people have endured for the motherland . . . what in the world are you thinking?"

"Princess Sophia Augusta Fredericka of Anadalt-Zerbst, Germany," Peter sneered, pronouncing each word with precision, "Your mendacity, like your many slips, is showing."

"You question my sincerity? How so? I've fully upheld my part of the bargain. When Czarina Elizabeth commissioned me to marry you, I dutifully learned the language, the history, and accepted the Russian Orthodox church. So committed was I to my task, I even took a new name for myself. I *became* Russian, and now, I love Russia!"

Sensing the sudden tension in the room, Ivan began jumping up and down, nattering nervously.

"Ivan, be quiet!" commanded the czar, but to no avail. The little monkey was used to doing exactly as he pleased, knowing full well that he was the family's palace favorite.

Ignoring the rambunctious animal, Peter took his wife to task.

"Ah, yes. And what have you done since becoming a patriotic Russian? I'll tell you. You have gone on one non-stop buying spree, that's what."

"I have--"

"For example," Peter thundered. "Not only did you purchase that Frenchman Diderot's Encyclopedia, but you are still paying him for more compilations." Peter waved the violin bow angrily above his head. "Did you know that Diderot was in this very room earlier today blubbering that he needs his friend Voltaire to come here and assist him? So right now the esteemed Monsieur Voltaire is enroute from Paris--at *my* considerable expense--to help your friend organize the forty thousand books in the palace library *you* purchased because you said you just *had* to have them."

"If Monsieur Diderot is having difficulty organizing his materials, he should have come to me," Catherine countered, squeezing Ivan's hand in an unconscious bid for support. "I would have given him more space for his research papers."

"Where? You already have rooms jammed with paintings and drawings. The servants have converted one entire room into a giant jewelry box filled with your cameos, engraved gems, necklaces, earrings, and bangles."

"You don't understand." The empress spread her arms wide as if commanding attention from the universe. "My so-called buying sprees are *us* telling the world that Russia is a center of culture and civility."

"Hah! I think you're just trying to impress the boyars with all your coins and medals and porcelains and tapestries. Now, since you've begun writing comic plays, I suppose you'll want a special room for your manuscripts and maybe even a private theater. Well, I'm getting tired of you playing palace all the time, and I'm getting tired indulging your never-ending whims."

"*Playing*?" Catherine sputtered. The empress could barely contain her frustration. "In case you haven't noticed, you and I have the responsibility of protecting and building the motherland, and part of that includes 'playing palace', whether you like it or not."

By now, Ivan was becoming both hungry and bored. He tugged at his mistress's dress, attempting to pull her toward the door. Catherine ignored the primate, instead focusing her attention solely on her husband.

"Don't lecture me about responsibility," Peter declared haughtily. "I've been Czar less than six months, and I've already enacted over two hundred laws, established a state bank, abolished the secret police, and mandated that the aristocrats educate their children. I've worked hard. So hard, in fact, that I deserve a holiday, and I intend to take one."

"Very well, Peter. I'm tired arguing with you. By all means, take a vacation. But before you depart, don't forget; my monthly masquerade ball is tonight, and I expect you to attend."

"But of course," the czar sniggered. "The servants tell me you have something new cooked up. The men will all dress as women and the women will dress as men. It should make for an interesting evening. Luckily, my panniered gown is clean and hanging in the closet."

Turning his back to Catherine in a clear gesture of dismissal, Peter lifted his violin to his shoulder and made his way to a window in a far corner of the room. There he began sawing away on the instrument, producing a series of loud and distinctly unpleasant screeches. Ivan smacked his own ears in protest, then scurried behind Catherine as the two of them beat a hasty retreat from the czar's chamber.

As soon as they were gone, the czar ceased sawing on his violin. Facing the chamber door, hands and violin at his hips, Czar Peter the Third of Russia stuck out his tongue in childish, but oh-so-gratifying defiance.

CHAPTER SEVEN

Catherine rapped on the door to her apartment. As she did so, Ivan, impatient for his food, squawked and screeched.

"It's your empress! Open the door!" she commanded, a steely ring of authority in her voice. Two stocky servant women pushed the door outward.

"So good to see you home, my Empress. Your meal and guests await you."

Masking her annoyance from her encounter with the czar, Catherine smiled and nodded. Stepping forward into the commodious chamber, Catherine was reunited with her son, Paul. He skipped toward his mother with Gracie in his arms, who was now adorned in an emerald satin and lace gown. Paul exclaimed, "Mama! Look what Paprika wants to give Grandpa Peter."

Paul held out a piece of paper to his mother. Princess Dashkova winked at Catherine, and the two servant women beamed with pleasure. Meanwhile, Ivan peered intently at the unfamiliar tiny creature, its tail protruding from an opening in the exquisite garment.

Noting Ivan's teeth and wondering what might be coming next, Gibson tensed as he rested on Orlov's lap. The general himself, curious as to what Ivan's reaction to Gracie and Gibson would be, adjusted the collar of his uniform. Reaching for the paper, Catherine asked, "What is this, Paul? What does Paprika wish to give Grandpapa?" Catherine studied the document and beheld a jumble of inky paw prints.

Turning to her son, Catherine asked, "Dear, please tell me what the letter says. I'm afraid I don't understand Paprika's writing."

"The letter," Paul declared, "says from Paprika the First to Peter the Great, with love."

Catherine gasped in mock astonishment. "Why, indeed it does!" she cried while noting a nearby table overlaid with layers of smudged paper and one enormous saucer filled with black ink.

Viewing the empress's quizzical expression, Princess Dashkova quickly set matters straight.

"My Royal Empress, we made certain little Paprika wrote her letter *before* we adorned her in your precious doll's dress." Young Paul nodded in eager agreement.

Pleased, Catherine said, "Paul, mama has an idea." She deftly lifted Paul and Gracie to her bosom and marched to an enormous marble fireplace, above which hung a magnificent painting of the late Czar Peter, brushed in deep hues.

Catherine said, "Why don't we place Paprika's letter on the mantel so Grandpa and Paprika can get to know each other?"

Gracie chirped her approval. While waiting for the empress to return to her apartment, Gracie had listened to Paul regale the adults with tales of his handsome great grandfather's many escapades. She knew that the monarch was highly esteemed by his countrymen.

Ivan, unsure as to what he was witnessing, rambled over and seated himself on a dining chair next to Orlov. Gibson, his tail twitching, squirmed on the general's knee; his unblinking eyes viewed Ivan with suspicion.

Princess Dashkova announced, "My Royal Empress, the food is on the table. Won't you and Paul join us?"

Catherine lowered Paul to the floor. Paul took his mother's hand, beaming with happiness. Still clutching Gracie, he accompanied his mother to the dining area.

Catherine seated herself at the head of the table opposite Ivan. A generous plate of turnip and parsnip greens awaited Gracie. Because she was too tiny to sit in a chair, Paul positioned Gracie atop the table near his mother. Famished, Gracie immediately began nibbling at the mound of greens with appreciative gusto.

Orlov deposited Gibson in a chair next to Gracie. Stretching his long body, the cat rested his paws on the table, and savored a meal of caviar, buttered bread, and a bowl of milk. The adults dug into their meal of sausages and dumplings, and began talking of palace gossip and the events of the day.

When Paul finished his plate, one of the serving ladies placed a small bag on the table in front of the child. Gibson noticed that the boy didn't seem the least bit surprised by the bag's appearance. Curious as to what it contained, Gibson decided to attempt conversation with the monkey sitting at the head of the table.

"Excuse me. My name is Gibson, and the creature munching the greens is my friend, Gracie. What's your name?"

Gracie lifted her head from the plate just long enough to acknowledge Ivan, then resumed chowing down.

The monkey swallowed a piece of apple and said, "My name's Ivan. Around here I'm known as Ivan the Terror."

Gracie ceased her munching and looked up. "Why are you called Ivan the Terror?" she asked.

"Why do you think, you little sausage?" Ivan replied, making a clear reference to Gracie's robust girth.

"That's no way to speak to my friend," Gibson admonished, his ears angling back. "I suggest you mind your manners."

Ignoring Gibson, Ivan declared, "I bore easily. When I'm bored, I'm mean." Reaching into Paul's bag, Ivan continued, "I also need constant attention."

"Ivan, keep your hands off Grandpa's teeth," little Paul scolded. Paul pulled the bag closer to himself. Ivan snorted his displeasure, flashed his teeth defiantly, then dipped his apple into a bowl of honey before gobbling it down.

"Ivan, is that bag really full of Peter the Great's teeth?" Gracie asked, incredulous at the thought.

"No, Sausage, that bag doesn't hold Czar Peter's teeth; that bag holds the czar's *collection* of teeth, the teeth he pulled in his lifetime."

"Was Peter the Great a dentist before he became czar?"

"I suppose you could say that. The man wore many hats."

Gibson's ears flicked forward. "We want to learn more about Peter," he said.

"What can you tell us about him?"

Ivan paused, knowing he had a rapt audience now.

"Did you hear Paul relating his great grandfather's accomplishments to Orlov and the princess before dinner?"

Yes, Gracie nodded. She remembered.

"Telling stories about grandpa is Paul's favorite pastime."

"I didn't hear the stories," Gibson declared, "I was busy playing with the General. Would you mind repeating them?"

"Only if you give me your full attention," Ivan insisted.

"We will. We promise," Gracie said.

Savoring the feeling of self-importance that his knowledge gave him, Ivan began,

"The old grandfather stood at least six foot eight in his *valenkies*."

"His what?" Gibson asked.

"His boots," the primate clarified.

Gracie tried to imagine Peter standing before their table. Imposing didn't begin to describe how he must have appeared.

"Peter's curiosity knew no limit," Ivan went on. "Before he came to the throne, he even studied astronomy."

"The stars!" Gracie chimed gleefully. "I've studied astronomy, too."

"Sausage, your full attention, please!" Ivan chided.

Gracie lowered her head in deference. Ivan cleared his

throat before continuing.

"There wasn't anything Czar Peter couldn't do. He knew how to cast metal, build a boat, make sails, and shave a face. If someone complained of a loose tooth, Peter would personally relieve him of the offending chopper."

"Mr. Ivan," Gracie interrupted, "May I ask a question?"

"You may."

"Could you explain to us what Master Paul *does* with his great grandfather's collection of teeth?"

"Look at the boy now and see for yourself."

While the adults dined and talked amongst themselves, young Paul was utilizing the teeth as counting beans, tutoring himself in the relationship of one numeric quantity against another.

Gracie was impressed. So, too, was Gibson, but he cautioned himself to presume nothing after just one day in the eighteenth century. He looked back at the painting of Czar Peter hanging above the mantel, and to his astonishment, then dismay, Gibson saw the long departed Czar smile and boldly wink directly at him.

"*Oh, no,*" Gibson thought, a shudder running through his body.

He slowly turned to Gracie, and in a dejected voice announced, "They're back. My visions are back."

Gracie didn't know whether to be concerned or not. "I wouldn't worry," she counseled. "We'll figure out a way to get back to the twentieth century. I'm sure once things are normal again your visions will disappear." She hesitated for a moment, then unexpectedly giggled. "On the other hand, I have to admit I'd actually like to meet Peter the Great . . .

Wouldn't you?"

They both laughed in an attempt to make light of this unexpected development. Ivan said nothing, but as he reached for another apple, he vowed to keep a close eye on these two interlopers.

CHAPTER EIGHT

Clearing his throat, Ivan the Terror reclaimed Gracie and Gibson's attention.

"It would serve you both to know who I am and what you are dealing with."

"Oh?" said Gibson.

Ivan explained. "I'm from Afghanistan, where I lived in a palace with a sultan. In other words, I'm used to the finer things in life. A Russian ambassador thought I would make an excellent present for the czar. The sultan sold me at a substantial profit, and here I am, the czar's favorite possession, living in a city of monumental splendor."

Gibson took in this information as he lowered his head to the bowl of milk and began slurping up tiny mouthfuls.

Gracie fixed her gaze on Czar Peter's collection of teeth and pondered the implications of Ivan's high status in the palace pecking order.

The monkey glowed with self-satisfaction. "In case you don't get it, let me clue you in. I get away with anything I want. The czar, the empress, and little Paul think I'm cute as a bunny. Stay clear of my bad side, or else Sausage here will end up as a curiosity in the menagerie across town; and you, oh great black panther, will be a common palace cat, eking out an existence hunting rodents."

"Mr. Ivan," Gracie ventured, "we want nothing more

than to return home. Will you help us? If we can get back to the post office, I assure you we'll be gone."

"Gone where?"

"In a few days, we should have a ride waiting for us," Gibson answered quietly. "Then it's back to, well, I don't think you'd understand."

"We want to return to another dimension," Gracie explained. "*Our* dimension--in the twentieth century. This is the eighteenth century, and I think you'll agree, we're a bit out of our element here."

Another dimension, another century--the concepts were beyond Ivan's comprehension.

Inquisitive though, Ivan asked, "What's happening *now* in your twentieth century"

"I don't know about this town, but the big news is that your country has launched an orb to the cosmos. It's called *Sputnik*. We hear your country is now working on sending dogs on a space voyage."

"Dogs?" Ivan snorted in disgust. "What about monkeys?"

"Cape Canaveral--that's in our country--is working with monkeys," Gibson answered.

"What if I showed up at Cape Canaveral? I've always wanted to see the stars and fly across the sky."

Gibson would have gladly granted Ivan his wish.

"If it were possible," he said, "I'm sure you would be considered. But it's just not possible; you belong here, and we belong there."

Gracie added, "There's not enough room in our

transport for the three of us. But even if there were, we don't have the connections to assist you if you made it to Cape Canaveral. You'd be completely on your own in a different time and in a strange country."

Ivan eyed his dish of honey. For him the answer was easy: given the choice of flying in space or enjoying his daily palace repasts, he'd take the honey every time.

CHAPTER NINE

"Listen."

Catherine's command silenced all conversation. Paul ceased counting teeth, and Ivan momentarily ignored his honey-dipped apples. Gibson and Gracie looked intently at one another. Both wondered, *Now what*? The sound they heard was a loud banging coming from the foyer.

The empress directed her servants to open the door. "That must be Diderot," she explained. "I forgot all about the poor man. This is his usual time of day to visit."

Anna and Ulyana hurried to open the massive door. Waiting on the other side was Doctor Orreus, the palace physician. Beside him stood the quivering, hunched Denis Diderot. Catherine stood up from the table, noticeably alarmed.

"My dear Empress . . ." began the physician.

"Gentlemen, do enter; both of you," Catherine said.

The men slowly entered the room. Dr. Orreus, well aware of the empress's proclivity for socializing with unusual characters, focused his attention solely on the sovereign, politely ignoring Ivan and the two furry additions to the empress's circle of friends.

"Monsieur Diderot, are you not well?" Catherine inquired, noting her dear friend's pale face.

"Your highness, I am here on behalf of my good friend Denis," Dr. Orreus replied. "I'm afraid he has worked himself to near exhaustion and urgently needs to get away for a few days."

Diderot nodded for the doctor to continue.

"I have volunteered to keep a close eye on Monsieur for the next few days--with Czar Peter's permission, of course. When we return, our friend's constitution should be renewed and his vigor restored."

"That won't be a problem," Catherine declared generously. "Your health is my primary concern, though of course I'll regret missing our discourses on philosophy." Catherine shook her head sadly. "Must you leave immediately?"

"I'm afraid so," Dr. Orreus confirmed.

"Then I shall miss both of you at tonight's masquerade ball. Such a pity."

Diderot and the doctor glanced at one another, clearing their throats.

By way of apology, Diderot declared, "We would never miss such a splendid event if it weren't necessary, my Empress." Bowing his head solemnly, he offered a book to the empress.

"Before I go, allow me to present you this volume by Plato. I catalogued it only this morning and I know he's one of your favorites. I've earmarked certain passages that I believe will be of interest to you."

"Why, thank you, Monsieur Diderot," Catherine replied, accepting the book by one of history's greatest philosophers.

Diderot, perspiring heavily, wiped his clammy forehead.

Looking up from his grandfather's collection of teeth, young Paul offered a cheery, "Enjoy yourselves, Monsieurs. Bring back some good stories; my friends love good stories."

The general and the princess smiled approvingly at the two men. The physician and the encyclopediest bowed respectfully, then, eager to be gone, locked arms and quickly took their leave.

Returning to her chair, Catherine's pinched brow revealed concern for her scholarly friend. He was one of the few men in her world who challenged her intellect.

The woman wondered if her passion for collecting--and not just artworks but knowledge, as well--was indeed pushing Diderot to the edge, as her husband had warned. Catherine laid her new book on the table, and hoped that the man would return from his vacation revitalized.

Meanwhile, as the two men hurried down the palace corridor, they could barely contain their joy.

"Denis, my friend, we are going to have a vacation to remember! First, the dance hall, then billiards. Who knows where the night will end!"

"You freed me from that prison of a library for an entire weekend!" Diderot exclaimed.

"Not to mention, I freed us from the masquerade ball, boring conversations, and those small-minded boyars with their oversized egos."

"Oh, the providence of St. Petersburg is shining upon us!" shouted Diderot. As the men danced down the corridor, Czar Peter poked his head outside his apartment door. Watching the two men gleefully descend the stairs, Peter cracked a wide grin. He had granted them their requested leave earlier this morning, and that act now made *him* feel good. In fact, he realized with a start, for some strange reason he now felt better than he had in a very long time.

CHAPTER TEN

Seeing Anna place a bowl of raw egg whites on the table for Catherine and the Princess, General Orlov said, "My Empress, the food was delicious. I believe it is now time for the gentlemen to depart. Would master Paul wish to accompany me to the billiard room?"

Paul nodded eagerly, and the empress said, "So kind of you, General."

Orlov reached down and scratched Gibson's ear. Seated like a lion protecting his territory, Gibson's tail rose and fell like a giant feather.

Turning to Gracie, the general patted the top of her tiny head. "Maybe you're not so bad, after all, little Flatfoot," Orlov admitted.

Gracie, who was still working on her plate of greens, playfully fluttered her eye-lashes.

The general, with young Paul in tow, pointedly ignored Ivan as they left the room. Orlov was eager to teach Paul billiards, and Paul was just as eager to learn.

Vowing not to forget the general's deliberate snub, Ivan scrambled to a nearby chaise lounge. Sprawling atop the velvet seat, he daydreamed about the land where he had been born. A caged bird elsewhere in the room cooed the monkey to sleep, although it was a slumber punctuated by unceasing grunts and snores.

Freed of the men, Catherine and the princess dipped their fingers into the porcelain bowl of egg whites and gently patted the goo on their faces. The servant women, used to the routine, carried in a pair of leather ottomans. Adjusting their feet atop the stools, both women settled comfortably into their chairs.

Catherine said, "Ulyana, please bring Paprika to me. I want to hold her."

Gracie found herself suspended high in the air, feet dangling, then just as quickly plunked down onto the empress's ample bosom. Dotingly, Catherine wiped a smidgen of egg from her face and bestowed the glop on Gracie's nose.

Wanting to be near Gracie, Gibson sprang from his chair. He glided over to the empress and placed both paws on the woman's lap.

With her free hand, the empress stroked Gibson's head. Soon both women and 'roo were relaxing to the sound of Gibson's contented purr.

Eyes closed, Catherine addressed her captive audience.

In a trancelike voice, she said, "You know, I consider myself a rather noteworthy personage, and I have great plans for Russia." The features of her face, even from behind the clown-like mask of egg whites, revealed a woman who was fully confident of her ability to succeed at any task. Lifting her chest and releasing a deep sigh, she declared, "I shall be a role model beyond compare."

Warming to her own vision of herself, the empress went on, "Because of my example, perhaps someday, in every nation, women will vote." She glanced down at Gracie and was warmed by the 'roo's unwavering attention. "Yes, my plump little

Paprika," Catherine murmured, dabbing her finger against Gracie's sticky nose. "Even in my beloved Russia women will vote." Gracie snuggled closer to Catherine. She was mesmerized, though more by the empress's comforting heartbeat than by the words.

Lifting her finger from the 'roo's nose, the empress abruptly ended her reverie.

"But not now," she declared emphatically." It's too soon for all that now. There's still too much to do, too many buildings, roads, and hospitals to build. Voting rights and my people's freedom will have to wait."

Anna and Ulyana glanced furtively at one another, shaking their heads. If there was so much to do, the women wondered, why must the people still wait for a little freedom? Gibson took this moment to slide his paws from Catherine's lap, and drop his front feet to the floor. He couldn't totally relax knowing that he and Gracie didn't belong in this time and place. Here, even a cat had to constantly look over his shoulder and expect the unexpected.

Catherine suddenly bolted forward in her chair. "Speaking of what Russia needs, Ulyana, what happened to my three R's?"

"My Royal Empress, the Rembrandt, the Rubens, and the Raphael paintings you ordered are temporarily stored at the Peter and Paul Cathedral," the portly peasant woman explained. "The servants are trying to find room for the paintings here in the palace."

"Find room? One would think that any palace capable of holding three thousand guests in the main ballroom would have plenty of room!"

"Yes, my royal empress, one would certainly think so," Princess Dashkova agreed tactfully.

Then, wanting to re-direct Catherine's attention, she asked, "What passage from Plato do you think Monsieur Diderot wants to thrash out with you? Not that it would make the least bit of sense to me."

Catherine reached for the book. Still disappointed about the paintings, she leafed through the pages until she came to the passage Diderot had marked. Catherine took a moment to read the great philosopher's words. Without speaking, she closed the tome and returned it to the table, her brow furrowed, her lips pouting.

"What does the passage say?" Princess Dashkova asked.

"It says . . . It says 'Do nothing in excess.'" Genuinely upset by this unequivocal rebuke, Catherine thought, *Who does Diderot think he is?*

"It's not *my* fault he can't get his precious encyclopedia organized," she exclaimed heatedly. "And if anyone thinks I'm going to stop my purchases just because Diderot, Czar Peter, and Plato disagree with my thinking, then they are badly mistaken!"

Fueled by an upwelling of manic anger, the empress shouted, "I am Empress of Russia, and I'll do as I please!" Then, unable to control her rage, she grabbed the offending book and hurled it against the wall. It tumbled to the floor, its brittle spine fracturing like a broken limb.

Gracie hopped over to inspect the pages that were loosened from the binder. Catherine, her face still flushed, suddenly experienced a rare sense of remorse. She had damaged a valuable item--a rare book that had no doubt cost her a pretty ruble.

Not smart, she chided herself. Her rage now cooled as quickly as it had ignited. The empress noticed Gracie jumping up and down next to a piece of paper that had come free from the book.

"What is it, Paprika? Are you trying to tell your matiushka something?"

Catherine went over and plucked the paper off the floor. It wasn't a page that had come loose, but a sheet of paper that had been tucked between the pages. She studied it carefully, then held it to the light. Imprinted on the fine vellum sheet was a detailed rendering of what appeared to be a large palace--except the handwriting, in French, identified it as a museum in Paris. Catherine stared at the drawing. She was enchanted, not only by the sheer beauty of what was portrayed, but because there was something else here, too. Something spoke to her . . . there was a message that only she--the Empress of Russia--could decipher. She pondered what it might be. . . and then she knew. It was obvious.

"Of course!" she exclaimed, thrilled by her own creative insight. "What a brilliant idea! What good will it be for my beloved Russia if only the nobles can view the treasures I'll amass over the years? If St. Petersburg had a museum, everyone could enjoy and appreciate the splendors of our empire." Catherine spun around and addressed the princess. "Yes! Diderot, naïve though he may be, must continue his work. We will classify, sort, and label everything, down to the smallest knickknack so that someday all of Russia, if not the world, will marvel at our exemplary taste and sophistication."

"You will bring culture to our people," Princess Daskova declared. "That is truly a noble undertaking."

"The task before us will require much time, patience, and thought. I'll be too busy organizing things here to shop--which, if nothing else should make Peter and Diderot happy." Catherine raised her egg-whited face dramatically to the heavens, "Plato will have to eat his words. My excess will lead the people of Russia to a glorious future, and they'll thank me for it many times over."

Instinctively, Gibson looked up too--not to the heavens, but to the ceiling. There, to his astonishment was that man again. Suspended in space, Grandpa Peter the Great smiled mischievously, and winked yet again at the by now deeply perplexed Gibson. As the cat watched, the long deceased ruler of Russia threw back his head and treated himself to a hearty, if soundless, paroxysm of laughter.

CHAPTER ELEVEN

As they chattered away in Catherine's apartment, the women realized that transforming the Winter Palace into a museum would be a formidable task.

"Should I hire a decorator or should I do it myself?" Catherine wondered aloud.

"Hire someone!" exclaimed Anna, Ulyana, and the Princess in unison.

"We need you to help lead the empire," the princess counseled. "Establishing a museum will be a full-time job in itself."

"You're right," Catherine agreed. "If I'm to get anything done, I must view time as a valuable commodity."

As the women continued their discussion, Gibson and Gracie huddled down beneath the chaise lounge. There, feeling a sense of security, the friends discussed their plight.

"I'm beginning to feel like a captive zoo animal," Gibson muttered.

"There has to be a way out of here," Gracie said. "We'll be free if we just stay positive."

Still napping, Ivan snorted and snored away like a broken locomotive.

Suddenly, the czar's booming voice shattered the tranquity of the moment. A barrage of heavy knocks on the door caught everyone's attention.

"Catherine! Open the door! I need your help."

Working quickly, Anna and Ulyana opened the portal, then stood back as the ruler of Russia made his entrance-- all white hosiery, purple silk briefs, and corkscrew chest hair protruding from a delicate lace camisole.

Oblivious to his less-than-regal appearance, Peter said, "Catherine, do you or any of your flapping hens have a wire cage for my panniered dress? That is, if your masquerade ball is still on for tonight."

"Of course it is," Catherine replied. "Anna, Ulyana, Princess--please fetch the rooster his cage."

Once the women departed, Peter became serious. "Catherine," he said, "please listen. I have something important to tell you. I'm tired of playing palace. I don't want to be a czar anymore."

Shocked, Catherine stood motionless while she gathered her wits. When she spoke, it was in a gentle, reasonable tone. "What is it you'd rather do, Peter? If not czar . . ."

"I wish to return to my family in Prussia and live out my life as the Duke of Holstein."

Gracie and Gibson's ears perked up when they heard "Holstein." They remembered that Farmer Heinselman had many black-and-white Holstein cows on his Pennsylvania farm, the place they had first met just a few months ago. The word Holstein made Gracie homesick for the farm, and her doldrums only deepened as the royal couple continued their bickering.

"Peter," Catherine scolded, "your auntie adopted you.

Providence dictates that you should be czar."

Peter clenched his fists and stamped his feet. "Why couldn't providence dictate that I drive a troika of horses? Now there's a job worth having."

"If you'd like--and *only* if you'd like--I'd be willing to assist you in your duties more than I presently do. Would that make things easier for you?"

The czar pondered Catherine's proposal and imagined what would happen if he granted his wife greater control and responsibility for the affairs of the palace. His mind's eye envisioned sacks of dazzling broaches, buckets of pearl necklaces, acres of bronze statues, and rooms full of German furniture. He imagined Diderot on his knees pleading for relief from the unrelenting tidal wave of books and antiquities that were toppling down over the encyclopedist's slender frame.

"Interesting idea," he mumbled. "We'll discuss it later. Meanwhile, have Ulyana bring the cage to my chamber."

As he turned to leave, more knocks sounded on the door, knocks that quickly escalated to an insistent pounding. The clatter of clomping hooves could be heard coming from the hallway. The czar looked at his wife and asked, "What the devil is that?"

"It must be Brilliant," Catherine cried happily as she rushed to open the massive door. Tall, handsome, and stately, Brilliant clopped through the open doorway led by a uniformed manservant. The white horse, attired in his finest gear, nuzzled Catherine's neck and bosom.

Awakened by the racket, Ivan sprang from his lounge chair. Immediately he began to tug on the equine's tail.

Gibson licked Gracie's head, and murmured, "Things

are getting really crazy around here."

This was confirmed by the czar, who said, "Ah, let me guess, Catherine. Brilliant is here to accompany you to the ball. Correct?"

"Can you think of a better way for me to make a grand entrance? I'll sit atop this magnificent stallion, a sword in my hand, dressed as a colonel of the Preobrazhensky Guard."

"You'll be perfect in the part," the czar deadpanned.

By now Ulyana had returned with the wire frame for the czar's dress.

He took the apparatus from the servant and murmured to Catherine, "I need some rest. I'll see you tonight." Slipping past Ivan, who was trying to swing from Brilliant's tail, Peter hastened out the door, leaving it slightly ajar.

"Gracie," Gibson whispered, "now's our chance. Let's go." He clamped down on Gracie's neck, picked her up and trotted out the door. Loping down the corridor, he made it past the buttress forming an alcove in the vestibule that shielded them from the czar's barking dogs.

"Hey, wait for me," Ivan shouted, coming up from behind. "You'll get caught if you go down those steps."

Gibson, heeding the monkey's advice, came up short and slid into a marble statue. Gracie sprawled to the floor.

Shaken, but unharmed, Gracie picked herself up and asked, "Mr. Ivan, what do you suggest we do?"

"Follow me," the monkey instructed.

Gibson once again gathered up Gracie and followed Ivan down the hall. Ivan stopped in front of the czar's chamber door. Gibson lowered Gracie gently to the floor and asked, "Why are we stopping here? Isn't this the czar's . . ."

"Relax," said the monkey. "In a few minutes, he'll be sleeping like a baby. Besides, his bed is in the back room. He's been known to snooze right through the merrymaking. The empress is still going gaga over Brilliant, and then she'll take a long bath. That means we're free to do as we please."

"But I don't understand why we want to go into his room," Gracie said.

"The best way to get out of here without being noticed is from the czar's chamber. Just follow me. I'll explain."

Ivan led the way through a small hinged door that had been installed especially for him. Once inside the apartment, he said, "Maybe if you're lucky you'll find the secret passage leading from here to the courtyard. I remember seeing it when I was brought here as a baby."

"What do you mean, 'if we're lucky'?" Gibson asked, suddenly skeptical.

"It's up to you to find the passageway. I'm here because I want to get dressed for the ball," Ivan declared. "Plus I also want more dessert."

"Gibson," Gracie whispered, "Ivan just ate with the rest of us." Curious, but saying nothing, Gibson tilted his head.

"After I've eaten," the monkey said, "I might help you find the opening. After all, your departure wouldn't bother me in the least."

Hmm, Gracie thought, *we can always count on good ol' Ivan. What a swell monkey.*

"Now, if you'll excuse me," Ivan went on, "I have things to do. Starting with this."

"With what?" Gibson asked.

"Just watch. I'm sure you'll find it pretty amazing, if I do say so myself."

With that, Ivan leaped up onto a marble credenza and grabbed a long candle snuffer. From there he scaled a bookcase. At the summit, Ivan leaped into the air and took hold of a brass chandelier as if it were a jungle vine. He swung fearlessly to the far side of the room and dipped the candle snuffer into a golden ooze that was running in folds down the wall. The ooze was almost invisible because the walls were blanketed in a veil of amber. Deftly, Ivan stuck the sharp end of the snuffer into the thick, sticky fluid. Then he popped the silver stick into his mouth.

Smacking his monkey lips as though he were sampling a fine wine, Ivan shouted, "I love honey!" Then, after pushing his body forward to gain momentum, he swung backward in preparation for another dive into the golden treat.

"This is so grand!" he sang rapturously.

Gibson turned to Gracie and said, "Do you believe what we're seeing?"

"Unfortunately, yes. But the question is, what do we do now?"

"Our only option is to look for the secret passage, although I happen to think that clown on the chandelier is playing us for fools."

The two of them began scratching and sniffing their way around the perimeter of the room. More than once Gracie pushed against the wooden baseboard beneath the dripping amber walls, but, to her growing consternation, nothing budged, wiggled, or indicated that escape from the palace was in any way possible.

CHAPTER TWELVE

Whack! Smack! Thump!

Deep in the rafters of the czar's chamber an angry sovereign from another kingdom inquired, "What's that sound?"

"My lady, it's Ivan again," Olga replied.

"I was sound asleep."

Concerned and hoping to comfort her queen, Olga said, "My queen, I've brought you a small snack. When you're finished, I'll scratch the mites away from your bed. You'll feel better."

Bam!

"That crazy monkey!" Queen Lidyia groaned. "He's giving me a headache."

"What can we do?" Olga sighed. "We did agree to a truce."

"Yes, but it wasn't fair, I had no choice. He was threatening to destroy us all."

The bees had made a pact with the palace terror. If they consented to his dipping into their delicious honey, the monkey promised not to reveal the bees' secret--that they were slowly taking over the palace.

"No one appreciates the sacrifices I've made," the

queen continued, her head throbbing. "For the good of the colony, I relinquished no small amount of my power to a yapping jungle creature." Ruing her plight, the queen bent over and sucked up a drop of liquid nourishment before continuing. "The drones and workers don't appreciate my responsibilities. Even on a *bad* day I've got to lay at least eight hundred eggs. It's no wonder I'm so stressed."

"But most days you manage to do fifteen hundred. That's quite impressive." Indeed it was, agreed the queen, although she much preferred being recognized for her unceasing self-sacrifice for the common good.

"Olga," directed the queen, "send out the drones to harass the pest. The monkey doesn't know they're incapable of harm."

Olga hesitated. "But your highness, doesn't the monkey know we agreed not to hurt him?"

"Yes, but he may think the drones have staged a coup," the queen explained. "Without me in command, he might assume they're incapable of being controlled." The sheer absurdity of the notion caused the queen's oversized body to quiver with delight. The surrounding bees picked up her vibration, and soon their sympathetic laughter turned into a steady low-level hum.

As the Queen's command filtered throughout the hive, the drones organized themselves for the mock attack on their nemesis. Meanwhile, worker bees returning home from a hard day in the fields collecting pollen and nectar talked amongst themselves.

"Oxana," complained one worker to a colleague, "does it ever end? In my entire lifetime I'll never produce more than one-twelfth of a teaspoon of honey. I have to ask myself, *what's the use?*"

"Never mind what we produce," Claudia advised, her four wings beating furiously. "All the queen cares about is our buzzing volume. If we're not flapping our wings 10,000 times a minute, the bosses think we're slacking off."

"This hive produced one pound of honey last week. We workers visited at least two million flowers, yet the queen's spies still monitor our buzzing. It's ridiculous, I tell you."

Claudia and Oxana, along with thousands of other worker bees, wearily made their way into the interior of the hive, hidden far up in the rafters of the palace. There they would grab a short nap, energizing themselves for the task of constructing honeycomb cells later in the evening. They weren't called worker bees for nothing.

Out in the amber room, Ivan noticed a growing swarm of drones hovering over his head.

Not the least bit intimidated by their presence, he inquired, "Hey, guys, what's up?"

"You're making too much noise," answered a drone.

"Yeah, you're upsetting our lady upstairs," declared a second bee, "and when she's unhappy, our lives are miserable."

"Oh? In what way?" Ivan asked, clinging to the chandelier.

"When she's unhappy, she makes us fix things--work, in other words, which is something we'd rather avoid."

A third bee, hearing scratching from below, glanced down at the floor. Not believing his eyes, he asked, "Am I hallucinating or is that rodent wearing a dress?"

All three bees now took notice of Gracie's emerald and lace attire.

"That is weird," said the first bee.

"And who's the cat?" asked the second bee.

"And why isn't the cat chasing the rodent," added the third bee, "instead of pawing at the czar's bookcase? What's it looking for?"

Before Ivan could supply the answers, the swarm heard a loud clattering from the rear of the czar's chamber.

"We'd better get out of here," declared bee number one. "The nincompoop is awake. We'll have to deal with the monkey later." With that, following a silent command, the entire squadron hightailed it up to the ceiling and made its way back to the hive, leaving Ivan dangling high above the floor.

CHAPTER THIRTEEN

Gracie worked her way around the perimeter of the room, kicking the floorboards, pulling at the moldings. By pressing against just the right spot, she hoped she would discover the door to the secret passage.

Melodious chamber music drifted up to the czar's apartment from the first floor ballroom. The music gave Ivan an idea. Tired of swinging, his passion for honey assuaged, Ivan decided to impress his captive feline and 'roo audience with a version of a dance step he had dubbed the Knuckle Walk.

Although the dance step turned out to be nothing more than a series of uncoordinated leaps, jumps, and monkey gyrations, it was enough to inspire Gibson to do a bit of high strutting on his own.

"Okay," he told Ivan, "now it's my turn. This is called the Cat Walk." Gibson lifted his head high in the air and pranced along the base of the bookcase as if he were a stallion. High in the rafters, the drones sensed the energetic dancing vibrations and decided that they, too, wanted in on the fun. Some drone bees displayed their well-practiced Round Dance skills, while others favored the Waggle. Worker bees laboring on the new comb cells joined the festivities, as well.

"Come on, Gracie," Gibson beckoned. "Ivan and I want to see your version of the Bunny Hop."

Gracie didn't answer.

Why didn't she answer? Gibson wondered. Feeling a wave of panic, Gibson cried out, "Gracie, where are you?"

"Sausage is asleep in the corner behind the screen over there," Ivan fibbed. He would say anything to gain his dancing partner's complete attention.

"Are you sure?"

"Yes," Ivan replied, pointing to a curled rat's tail jutting out from behind the screen at the far end of the room. Then he shouted, "Do it, cat!" while clapping his hands together and stomping his feet. "Ya feel the rhythm? Makes me want to swing and sway!"

Gibson couldn't feel any rhythm, but he had to admit he was having fun. The big cat picked up his paws and resumed prancing on the ledge of the bookcase.

Gracie, meanwhile, was anything but asleep behind the screen. Very much awake, amused and curious, she was hiding behind a marble statue. Her eyes were locked onto the figure of a bewigged man attired in white stockings, high heels, and purple underpants. Bent over, he was searching frantically through a large toy box. Gracie hopped closer, straining to hear what the man was saying.

"Here's my favorite general!" the czar exclaimed, placing the esteemed toy next to several other toy soldiers.

"Now, who wants to attend the ball?" he asked.

Silence.

"Don't you brave men have a tongue?" Peter demanded harshly. The czar awaited an answer. "Well then, who wants to play soldier?" The czar scooped up his playthings and shook them vigorously.

In a tiny childish voice, Peter declared, "*We* want to play soldier, Czar Peter."

"You do?" cried the emperor. "Splendid! So do I."

Gracie hopped closer still, wishing the Czar would include her in the fun. The mellifluous sounds of a waltz drifted through the czar's apartment, transforming the space into a warm and inviting refuge. The relaxed mood made Gracie want to say: "Mr. Czar, would you allow me to play with you?" But, of course, Gracie was unable to put this thought into words a human would understand.

Disregarding her most basic instincts, the 'roo jumped closer to Peter. Unable to restrain herself, Gracie hopped directly in front of him as if to say, *Here I am, Mr. Czar.* Lashes fluttering, Gracie held up her arms so the sovereign could lift her off the floor. Amused, Peter peered down at the 'roo.

"My little friend, what bit of luck brought *you* here?" Peter asked in genuine amazement. He plopped down in a chair, then lifted Gracie to his knees.

"Aren't you the pretty one! My son Paul told me we have a new curiosity in the palace." The czar scratched the back of Gracie's ear and said, "I'd rather spend an evening with you then with those stuffy boyars downstairs."

Knowing she commanded Peter's full attention, Gracie chirped and wagged her tail against his knee.

"Soldiers, the little princess wants to play with us," the czar announced, patting Gracie's head. "The soldiers say they want to play with you, too. We'll play spy. Curiosity, your dress is green, so you can be the spy since everyone here in my court must wear blue."

Peter carefully placed Gracie on the floor. On his knees

now, he delved into his toy chest, rummaging through the mishmash of items.

"Let's see. Here they are!" The czar plucked out a lace remnant and a feather.

"Little spy," said the czar, "you better tell me what you know." Gracie didn't understand what the czar meant, but she definitely wanted to be part of the action, so she didn't resist when the czar stood her against the leg of his bed. He wrapped the lace around the leg and Gracie's midsection making certain Gracie was comfortable.

"Tickle, tickle," he teased. "Tell Czar Peter what you know." The feather brushed across Gracie's throat almost imperceptibly. Gracie didn't understand, but she knew the silly man was having fun. With each stroke of the feather, Peter giggled.

When the czar giggled, Gracie chirped, reveling in her playtime romp. Lost in his fantasy, the czar failed to notice the worker bees gathering high above him.

"What is the nincompoop doing now?" asked the lead bee.

"I'm not sure, but I don't like what I see. We already know how he runs his poor dogs to exhaustion every afternoon. He must be torturing that little creature the same way he tortures his dogs."

"What do you care? It's only a rodent in a dress, pretending to be something it isn't. Rodents get what they deserve. You know that," said the leader.

"No creature deserves torture," countered the worker bee, "rodent or not."

Addressing Oxana, Claudia, and all the other hovering

bees, the second worker shouted, "Ladies, should we just swarm up here and pretend to see nothing, or is it time we teach the nincompoop a lesson?"

"Not so fast," cautioned the lead bee. "If you take on this mission, it'll mean the end of you."

Just then the czar deftly inserted the feather under Gracie's arm.

"Tickle, tickle, little rodent. Czar Peter wants to know where the boyars have hidden his marbles. Did the boyars steal them, or has the czar lost his marbles?"

Gracie laughed uncontrollably.

"Listen to that poor creature," wailed the second bee. "This outrage cries for action."

"You're right!" Oxana agreed." This mission shall give purpose to our existence."

"Wait!" cried the leader. "You'll be sacrificing your lives for a rat."

It was too late. Caution and reason were ignored. The second bee, then Oxana and Claudia flew up and under the czar's purple underpants.

"There go my best honey producers," moaned the leader bee. With each of the czar's blood-curdling screams, the courageous workers fell to the floor like acorns dropping from a tree, dead from losing their stingers.

Gracie, realizing that something was seriously amiss, quickly loosened the lace that held her to the bed leg. Gibson found her there, and, putting two and two together and coming up with five, decided to teach Gracie's perceived tormentor a lesson. He pounced on the back of the czar's purple behind, sliced through the silk fabric, and dug his claws into the czar's soft rump.

"Yeee-owl!" the czar screamed, his face grimacing in pain, his legs pumping up and down as if riding a bicycle. He pranced about the room, clutching his throbbing behind.

"Gibson, why did you do that?" Gracie demanded angrily. "We were just having fun."

Gibson, however, wasn't buying it; he continued to circle the czar, hissing and growling, boldly displaying his feline teeth. The lead bee applauded Gibson's action, but, knowing better than to push her luck, moved now to shepherd her bees back to the safety of the hive.

"Workers," she announced, "our mission is complete! The cat has entered the fray for round two." Actually, the lead bee simply didn't want to lose any more honey producers. Satisfied that they had taught the czar a well-deserved lesson, the bees dutifully fell into formation. Their pulsating wings lifted them to the ceiling, from which they returned to their hive.

"Gibson, please don't frighten the czar anymore," Gracie begged, only to have her pleas interrupted by the monkey.

Pleased and excited at finding Gibson and Gracie together, Ivan shouted, "Sausage, Feline, come quick! I've got--what's wrong with the czar?"

"He's in pain," Gracie wailed. "The bees stung him and I don't know why."

Gibson ceased circling Czar Peter, who flopped unceremoniously to the floor.

"Are you sure the czar wasn't hurting you?" Gibson asked.

Before Gracie could respond, Brilliant--preceded by a cacophony of clopping and snorting--shuffled into the room, nostrils flaring, ears thrust forward with Catherine astride his back. Dressed in a colonel's green uniform, she was wielding a long cavalry saber. General Orlov, attired in a décolleté dress, was at her side.

"Peter, we've come to fetch you. The boyars are asking embarrassing questions as to your--Goodness, what is going on here?"

"Matiushka," Peter blubbered, "some vile flying insects stung me." Tears streamed down his face and welts were beginning to appear under his quivering hands and fingers.

Just then, whether deliberately or quite by accident--no one could tell--Brilliant flicked his tail directly in Ivan's face. Before the monkey could even scream his outrage, the horse stepped sideways and delivered a quick back-footed kick to Ivan's behind. Howling more from surprise than pain, the palace terror began spinning and leaping about the room, as if mimicking the czar's own recent contortions.

Ignoring Ivan, General Orlov asked, "Czar Peter, are you in pain? There are red dots popping up all over your chest."

"I'm having trouble breathing," the czar wheezed.

To Gracie's horror, she saw welts forming all over his body.

"Orlov, summon Dr. Orreus," Catherine ordered.

"You won't find him," Peter said. "He and Diderot are out partying. At this very moment, Orreus is probably swinging from some post office chandelier."

"In that case, General, sound the alarm that the czar is sick and needs a doctor, any doctor."

"What should I say is wrong with him?"

"Tell them the czar is suffering from. . . hemorrhoids. Yes! Everyone knows he's had problems with them in the past."

Eyeing the numerous bee corpses on the floor, Catherine continued, "Whatever you do, don't say anything about bees. People mustn't know we've allowed them to infest the palace. They'll think we're idiots since everyone knows the czar is allergic to just about everything."

"Hurry, Orlov, it's getting harder to breathe," the czar gasped.

The general bustled out into the corridor, calling servants and militia to join him in the hunt for a doctor.

Catherine dismounted Brilliant and began wiping perspiration from the czar's forehead. Doing so, she noticed Gracie nibbling Peter's ear.

"Princess Paprika, I forgot all about you," Catherine declared. "I do hope you'll forgive me."

Attempting to pet Gracie, the czar struggled to speak in spite of his labored breathing.

"Perhaps you forgot about her because you have so much to remember. I mean, you must be very busy overseeing the scores of people required to run a palace, especially this palace."

"Peter, please, this isn't the time to--"

"This *is* the time, Catherine. I'm tired of being responsible for everything. *You* can oversee the architects and carpenters, the jewelers and silversmiths, and the all the engineers, shipbuilders, and generals that are needed to defend your precious collections."

"What do you propose to do, Peter?"

"If I make it through this scrape," he wheezed, "I'm taking a *long* hiatus from the palace. You can have it all. Nothing would make me happier than to be left alone so I can play in my own special sandbox."

"What sandbox? Is this something new?"

"That's my secret," the czar said in a pouting child-like voice.

Perplexed by her husband's words, Catherine caught sight of the lace remnant lying on the floor.

"What were you doing with this lace?" she asked, bending over to retrieve it.

"The Curiosity and I were playing spy. I used it to tie her to the bed leg."

The empress was aghast.

"You can't tie up an animal like that! Were you hurting her?" The queen pondered her suspicions. "People here in the palace already think you brutalize your dogs. Are you sure you took care not to hurt her?"

"Of course. I'd never hurt a little creature like that . . . or anything else, for that matter."

"Then why do your dogs howl all through the night? It's because they hate being pent up in cages, that's why. They need space, freedom, lots of it."

Realizing that perhaps he hadn't paid enough attention to his dogs' needs, the czar turned away, saying nothing. Feeling empathy for the man, Gracie nuzzled him gently above his ankle; Gibson, wanting to make amends for his earlier attack, placed a sympathetic paw on the sovereign's thigh, and purred his best purr.

Catherine stood, leaving Peter sitting cross-legged on the floor. She walked over to the portrait of Peter the Great, hoping the illustrious ancestor could provide her with a glimmer into her husband's behavior. She honestly couldn't understand why her husband didn't consider how animals felt. More importantly, she couldn't fathom how he or anyone could *not* want to be the czar of Russia.

Ivan, annoyed by the lack of attention he was receiving, limped over to Peter, Gibson and Gracie. "Listen," said the monkey, "what do I have to do, send you a letter? The two of you are as good as free."

"What do you mean?" Gracie asked.

"When the panther here jumped off the bookcase, his hind legs hit a set of books that aren't really books. They're fakes that are hiding the passageway I told you about. So now all you have to do is slip through the opening, trot down the stairs and you're out of here."

"Gracie, come on. Let's go."

Suddenly, the czar gasped for breath and fell onto his back, holding his fist to his chest.

"Gibson, look!" Gracie pointed. "The czar's welts are getting bigger. He's having so much trouble breathing, I wonder if . . . " Quickly, she reached into her pouch and pulled out her tiny bag of Get Well, Stay Well Stuff. Without hesitation, she sprinkled a few flakes on the ruler's heaving chest. "I should've thought of this before," Gracie said, admonishing herself. Almost immediately, like air leaking out of a beach ball, the welts withered into soft red blotches.

"Good work," Gibson declared. "Now, we really have to

get out of here."

As Gibson scooped up Gracie in his mouth, Ivan said, "Hey wait! What did Sausage sprinkle on the czar?"

The words had barely escaped his mouth when, with impeccable timing, Brilliant made a large deposit on the floor. With everyone distracted by the equine's all too horse-like action, Gracie and Gibson headed to the bookcase in search of the secret passageway that they hoped would lead them to their freedom.

CHAPTER FOURTEEN

The czar slept soundly in the sanctuary of his bed, relieved that he had escaped the foolishness of the masquerade ball. Exhausted from his encounter with the bees, Peter, in a white stocking cap and flowing cotton gown, lay under a sea of luxurious comforters.

Ivan was resting on the divan in the czar's front chamber, listless from gorging on too much honey, and sore from Brilliant's kick to his behind. Looking on the bright side, however, Ivan knew he had regained his position as the center of attention. He had helped Sausage and the feline escape. No one in the palace would know until it was too late that the duo was gone. The door to the secret passageway was now closed; Ivan had made sure of that.

Troubled, Catherine sat in a chair in her apartment sipping chamomile tea, clutching the lace that had bound Gracie to the leg of the bed. Her thoughts were interrupted by a knock on the door.

"Who is it?" the empress asked.

"Orlov."

"Please, come in, although you'll have to manage the door yourself. I told my servants I wished to be alone this evening."

The door creaked open. Now dressed as a general, Orlov stood at the entrance and bowed. Across the room, a silvery sheen of moon glow filtered through the palace windows, bathing Catherine in an icy, yet flattering radiance.

"My empress, Captain Marchenko and I never did find Dr. Orreus. Instead we dispatched Dr. Alexandervich."

"It doesn't matter, Orlov. The czar dismissed Dr. Aleandervich. Peter has recovered, and is asleep in his feathered bed. But I want to show you something. Please, look at this."

Puzzled, Orlov advanced, eying the lace that dangled from Catherine's outstretched hand.

"It is a fine piece of lace," Orlov declared. "What is its importance?"

"The czar said he was playing spy with Princess Paprika. He admitted that he used this very piece of lace to tie her to the leg of his bed. He said he was just playing, that he didn't do anything to hurt her."

"That's probably true. We both know the czar would rather play with toy soldiers than command real soldiers."

"Yes, but what about the way he treats his dogs? He boards them in that small makeshift alcove outside his chamber. He claims he wants to keep the dog house close by so that he can play *Chase the Squirrel* whenever he feels like it. He actually believes his palace hunting games are a secret, but I tell you, the entire palace knows about the dogs."

"I've no doubt you're correct."

"I wonder what else goes on in his chamber." Catherine clutched an exquisite peach-colored handkerchief. "If Peter ever hurt Paprika," Catherine continued, "I could no longer support him as Czar."

Orlov contemplated the lace hanging from Catherine's fingers. Could it be that the fate of the Russian empire might be determined by a piece of fabric and the well-being of a speckled, red-haired animal? It was mind-boggling.

Catherine interrupted Orlov's thoughts. "We'll also need to discuss this bee problem," she stated. "No one I've spoken to around here seems to have any idea where they are hiding. But, the bees can wait. It's been a long evening."

"I agree, my Empress. Until tomorrow, then."

The general bowed and left the chamber. In the dark and empty hallway, he whispered, "Captain Marchenko, are you still waiting for me?" From behind a marble column, out stepped Mikhail Marchenko. Still in his panniered dress, the Captain saluted Orlov.

"My friend, it's nearly dawn. Forget the formality. We need to address the problems that are threatening the motherland. It has been brought to my attention that our childish czar may be torturing the empress's new curiosity."

"General, just what is the new curiosity? Some say it is nothing more than an extraordinarily beautiful rat."

"Let's just say it is different. I've never seen such brown eyes and thick eyelashes on such a small creature. But the point is that if the Russian people thought their czar was torturing a helpless animal for sport, especially the empress's pet, they would definitely wonder about his fitness to command."

Captain Marchenko nodded knowingly. "Rumors . . ."

"Help the rumor along, Marchenko. We need to save the motherland."

"A good place to start might be the Post Office. I'm sure there are a few stragglers still partying."

"And, if the city's postmen get wind of the rumor, the information will fly all over town," Orlov added.

"With a little luck, people may even rush to the palace and demand that Catherine take over the reins of power. Perhaps neither she nor Peter will have a choice in the matter."

"If that were to occur, Captain, you and I would be the unsung heroes."

"For the motherland," Marchenko said, coming to attention in his fashionable dress.

"For the motherland," Orlov agreed.

CHAPTER FIFTEEN

Gibson's paw poked out from beneath the passageway door. It was half past three in the morning, and in the room, oblivious to Gibson's movements and accompanying grunts, Ivan lay snoring on a sofa. Hoping to attract attention-- anyone's--Gracie shoved a few flakes of her Get Well, Stay Well Stuff under the door. Though they sparkled and danced in the darkness, no one was around to take notice of the display. Everyone in the palace, it seemed, was asleep. No one saw or heard anything.

With only a hint of moon glow for illumination, Gibson and Gracie searched for a button that would allow them re-entry into the czar's chambers. As the duo went about their task, high above them worker bees flitted through the rafters, seeking new territory to add to their honey empire.

When the head worker bee and her entourage squeezed through a tiny crack in the ceiling, it sent sprinkles and spatters of plaster down upon Gibson and Gracie. Gracie, who was still attired in her emerald satin and lace dress, simultaneously squealed and hopped in surprise. "What was *that*?" she cried out in a loud whisper.

Zooming down to check out the commotion, the head worker bee quickly dispelled Gracie's fears. "Feline . . . Little Curiosity. What's wrong? Are you locked out?"

Gracie was eager to set the story straight.

"Gibson unlocked the secret passageway when he jumped off the bookshelf to rescue me," Gracie explained, "although actually the czar and I were just playing a game. He wasn't really hurting me."

The head bee said nothing. It distressed her to realize that she had lost some of her best honey producers due to a silly misunderstanding.

"When Ivan told us the passageway was open," Gracie continued, "Gibson and I ran down the stairway to escape. We wanted to go to the post office, but then we discovered that we had no way of opening the exit door or breaking a window."

"And by the time we got back upstairs," Gibson said, picking up the story, "Ivan had already closed the secret passageway, leaving us stranded down here."

"No problem," the bee declared, "I'll just tell Ivan to open the door--if that's what you really want."

"What do you mean?" Gibson asked.

"Well, you'll be back in the czar's apartment, yes . . . but you'll still be captives here in the palace."

"I know," said Gracie, "but at least the empress will take good care of us. Trying to survive on our own in this crazy kingdom . . . it might prove difficult."

"I hear you," said the bee.

"But, if an opportunity presents itself, like an open door and no one's around--we're outta here," Gibson clarified.

"Absolutely," Gracie agreed.

"In that case, I'll wake up Ivan," the bee declared as she retreated back up the stairwell.

Although they didn't know it, something very strange was occurring just then in the czar's chambers. Emanating from the dead bees which were scattered across the floor like weathered kernels of corn, shimmering beads of light hovered over each tiny body. Quickly, the light coalesced into a single large orb. The orb lifted higher and floated towards the portrait of Peter the Great. The flickering mass settled upon the great man's face, causing the czar's mustache to wiggle and his eyes to dart from side to side. Incredibly, the sleeping giant was awakening.

Also awakening, though very reluctantly, was Ivan.

"Get up, you lazy lump of meat!" shouted the chief worker bee. Stretching his limbs and yawning, Ivan rolled over on his side. "I said, wake up!" the bee barked.

Ivan slowly came to his senses. Visibly annoyed, he focused in on the bee and demanded, "What's going on? Why'd you get me up so early? The cooks probably haven't even started breakfast yet."

"Never mind breakfast," the bee declared. "Just listen. The feline and the curiosity couldn't open the exit door at the bottom of the passageway. They're tired, discouraged, and probably getting hungry; and they want back in. You're the only one who can open the passageway."

"Oh, yeah? Well, tell 'em I'm busy."

"Excuse me?"

"It takes a lot of energy to swing from that chandelier. In order to activate the door I have to bump up against the bookcase just right. I don't have enough strength yet. Tell 'em to wait until after breakfast." Concerned for Gracie and Gibson's well-being, the head bee said, "I suggest you don't make them wait too long."

"Why not?"

"Oh, you know . . . we have our ways of making things happen around here," the bee said flatly. In truth, the bee would have liked nothing more than to motivate Ivan with the same treatment the workers had meted out to the czar. Ivan, however, ignored the bee's implied threat and returned to the comfort of the sofa.

Infuriated by the monkey's laziness and insensitivity, the head bee gave a buzzing signal to her followers waiting high above. Immediately, they flew off to the hive, leaving Ivan alone with his monkey ruminations.

Concerned that Gibson and Gracie might feel abandoned, the bees quickly worked out a plan amongst themselves to supply their new friends with as much honey as necessary to keep the always worrisome threat of hunger at bay.

Meanwhile, as Gracie and Gibson consoled one another, and the czar and the empress slept, palace servants and worker bees alike prepared for the new day. Outside, as the hours ticked by and the sky lightened, peasants, cobblers, milkmen, water carriers, doctors, teachers and musicians slowly began congregating outside the palace walls.

The crowd was restive, though oddly silent. The collective mood was decidedly somber. Many of those now gathering carried large baskets stuffed full of savory sausage, dark bread, cheese and drink. To the many eyes peering out from the numerous palace windows, the meaning was crystal clear: the crowd was prepared to stay a while.

CHAPTER SIXTEEN

"Where is the empress?" General Orlov asked. His question was directed at Anna and Ulyana, who stood in the doorway like sentinels, their brows furrowed with worry.

"Is that you, general? Please, come in."

Catherine, Princess Dashkova, and Ivan were seated at a table piled high with breakfast rolls and meats. Though the repast was a visual delight, neither woman apparently had much of an appetite judging from the paucity of food on their plates.

As General Orlov made his way across the room, Catherine announced, "I have bad news, general."

"Yes, I-- "

"Princess Paprika is missing."

The general hesitated. Although he had far more weighty matters to discuss with her, he knew he couldn't afford to appear insensitive to Catherine's worries.

"I'm sorry to hear that," he replied in as comforting a tone as he could muster.

"What about Pepper? Is he--?"

"They're both gone and I miss them terribly. They were so innocent and pure . . ."

Catherine's eyes moistened, but her voice, when she

spoke again, was firm.

"Fate can be so cruel at times. However, now we must concern ourselves with the fate of the empire. Princess Dashkova and the servants have informed me that the crowd outside the palace is growing larger. What's to be done? I presume you've come up with a plan of action."

"Yes, Empress. We must remove the czar from the palace without the people's knowledge. So far, the crowd isn't showing its annoyance, but they are angry, to be sure. They've heard a vicious rumor that the czar was torturing a defenseless animal, your special pet curiosity, Paprika."

"Then they're right to be upset! Torturing animals is vile and despicable. I could never tolerate such behavior if it were true." What the queen feared most was her fear that perhaps whoever had spread the rumor had done so out of genuine knowledge, not malice or disloyalty. Not knowing the truth tore at her heart.

"For his own safety," Orlov continued, "we must remove the czar from the palace."

"I'm sure he'll agree. He's long wanted a vacation, so now he'll have his wish."

"How do you suggest we explain his absence?" asked the general.

"Use the hemorrhoid excuse. We'll say he's gone to recuperate at one of his hunting lodges. From there, you and your brother can smuggle him to any place he wants to go, as long as it's nowhere near here. I'll manage in his absence." Waving her napkin, Catherine went on, "I must tell you, General, my sense is that he'll never want to return. He loathes this place so much; he's always comparing Russia unfavorably to Prussia."

"Perhaps the people won't want him to come back."

She pondered this for a second. "That's very possible. Anyway, once you know he's safe and things have calmed down here, we'll arrange for Paul to visit him."

"We can utilize the secret passageway in his apartment to get him out of the palace," Orlov suggested.

"Excellent. It's always prudent to have an escape route handy. No ruler should be without one."

"Indeed so," Orlov agreed, "and, just to be safe, I'll make sure he wears a disguise in case anyone should spot us."

The queen nodded and sipped from her cup of strong tea. Ivan, however, most certainly did not agree with the plan. If Orlov and the czar escaped via the passageway, Ivan reasoned, *they would surely discover the feline and Sausage.* That would mean the two of them would be back in the palace, and Ivan wasn't about to share his privileged status with anyone. Ivan would have to get back to the czar's chambers unnoticed and help the pair run away.

While Catherine, Orlov, and Princess Dashkova hashed out the details of the czar's escape, Ivan slipped out the door behind Anna and Ulyana when the two servant women returned to the kitchen burdened with a load of dirty dishes. Anna and Ulyana didn't care where Ivan went as long as he stayed far away from them.

While Ivan scampered down the corridor, in an adjacent hallway the czar, still in his nightgown, and General Orlov's brother made their way to Catherine's quarters. The monkey pushed against the tiny trap door and gained entrance to the czar's apartment. He grabbed the candle snuffer, leaped atop the marble credenza and jumped up to gain hold of the chandelier. He swung on the light fixture until he had gained enough momentum to whack the bookcase in just the right spot.

The hidden door creaked open ever so slightly. Ivan slipped through the portal and was somewhat surprised to find Gracie and Gibson nowhere in sight.

He barreled down the steps shouting, "Feline, Sausage, where are you?"

"Down here," came a distant voice.

At the bottom of the stairs, Ivan found Gracie trying unsuccessfully to hit a thick grated window pane with her tiny body. Gibson lay exhausted on the floor, taking a break.

"Step aside and let an expert take out that window," Ivan declared.

More than willing to comply, Gracie did as requested. Ivan whacked at the window with all of his considerable might, but the glass was too well protected by its iron latticing. Challenged now, and highly motivated, the monkey continued to attack the tightly sealed porthole, which appeared to have been crafted out of colorful red, green, and yellow bottles. As he gathered his strength for a renewed assault with the candle snuffer, the three of them suddenly heard the unmistakable sound of the door slamming shut at the top of the stairs.

"Great," Gibson declared after a long pause. "Now we're trapped in here for good."

"No, we're not," Ivan countered. "If I don't show up for lunch, the empress will start looking for me. It's only a matter of time before we're rescued." The monkey puffed out his chest, full of confidence

I certainly hope so, Gibson thought as he swiped irritably at a large cockroach tickling his toes. *Bugs, spiders, filth--ugh! I'll take dining with the empress over this lifestyle any day."* He flashed what he hoped was an encouraging grin at Gracie. Always optimistic, Gracie returned his smile. Gibson then turned and padded up the stairs. With a little luck, he might find a plump mouse to dine on. It wouldn't be caviar, like last night, he knew, but surely it would taste just as fine.

CHAPTER SEVENTEEN

General Orlov and Captain Marchenko hastily ushered the czar, who was fashionably disguised as one of Catherine's ladies-in-waiting, away from the entrance to the secret passageway. After slamming the door shut, Orlov's brother hurried to the basement kitchen to see if their backup escape plan was still possible.

"Your Excellency, do you have any idea who might have opened the passageway door?" Orlov asked.

"No one knows about the door other than you, your brother, Catherine, and Captain Marchenko." The czar laughed, "Oh, and once when Ivan was still a baby, he saw Catherine enter my apartment through that passageway."

Ivan, thought General Orlov, *it's always Ivan when something goes amiss*. Then it occurred to the general: *By closing the door, had his brother inadvertently locked the mischievous monkey in the stairwell, and not some presumed spy?* A smile flashed across Orlov's face. *Perhaps in the spring I'll personally check out the secret passage. Since that's many months away, anyone--monkey or human--will be very dead by then. Pity.*

In the meantime, the general could look forward to the arrival of Grandfather Frost. Catherine had promised the boyars and officers that she would flood a portion of the palace grounds as soon as weather permitted so everyone could enjoy weekend ice skating parties.

A muffled bell clanged, interrupting the general's thought. The door of the dumbwaiter sprang open, and this time the large platform that usually held the czar's meals was empty.

"After you, Excellency."

Peter climbed onto the dumbwaiter, hugging his skirt and slips against his knees, leaving sparse room for Captain Marchenko to squeeze in beside him. The two men slowly descended to the kitchen where they were met by General Orlov's brother. The general himself joined them two minutes later. Once reunited among the pots and pans, the foursome skittered down yet another passageway, at the end of which, Captain Marchenko assured them, would be waiting a carriage and driver to spirit them away.

Even through the thick walls of the palace, the fleeing men could hear the rumblings of the massed citizenry. Copious amounts of food, drink and emotion were fueling the protesters' passions.

"We want Catherine! We want Catherine!" many shouted.

"Be kind to animals!" others proclaimed.

A third faction clamored, "Send the Holstein cow back to Prussia!"

Hours later, with the czar long gone and with the night still young, the rambunctious crowd was rewarded for its protestations. Inside the palace, Catherine, dressed in the green uniform of the Preobrazhenski Guard, mounted her white steed, Brilliant. Princess Dashkova lifted young Paul high in the air, allowing him to join his mother on top the horse. Surrounded by a milling retinue of boyars, military men, and a host of clergy, Catherine and Paul ascended the marble stairs astride the clopping Brilliant until they reached the magnificent open balcony at the top of the landing.

Before addressing the elated crowd, Catherine leaned down and said to Chancellor Voronstov, "I hope you understand. I'm only obeying the people's wish." Then, centering herself so all could see, Catherine held up her young son as if he were a trophy. The crowd cheered and roared its hearty approval.

There was, however, no joy in that forgotten wing of the palace where Gracie and Gibson now huddled together at the bottom of the stairwell. They were tired and frightened. *Would anyone ever miss them*? they wondered. *Would anyone ever find them?* Their sole source of light was the dim reflection of a distant outside lantern, and its faint rays did little to brighten the mood of the three prisoners. What they didn't know was that help was already on its way. It was--quite literally--in the air.

Upstairs, in the czar's chambers, tens of thousands of bees had massed together into a single swarm. They were pressing against the bookcase, searching for the spot that would release the door to the passageway.

Worker bee supervisors shouted commands: "Don't press each other too hard! Remember, if you get hurt our honey production will suffer, and we won't get our bonuses."

"Let's try again," bellowed the supreme leader of the worker bees. "When I say 'heave,' press the bookcase. Ready? Heave!"

The worker bees obediently followed orders, many falling to the ground, crushed by the mass of bodies, never to buzz again. If it was any consolation to them, however, their collective efforts this time succeeded, and the bookcase slowly opened. It took only a few seconds for a bee scout party to fly down the stairs and rouse the exhausted captives. Thanks to the light of the moon and stars shining through the apartment windows, the trio would be able to ascend the numerous stairs to the czar's chamber with little difficulty.

Ivan took off as if shot out of one of General Orlov's artillery pieces. Gibson, his instincts telling him that the monkey might be up to no good, grabbed Gracie in his mouth and bounded up the stairs. He entered the apartment just in time to spot Ivan already swinging from the chandelier. *What's he up to now?* Gibson wondered. Then, incredibly, a huge, long arm plucked Ivan off the lighting fixture and flung him to the floor. The arm belonged to a giant of a man sitting astride a horse that stood in the middle of the room.

Frozen with fright, Gibson--who was still clutching Gracie in his mouth--could only watch in disbelief as the horse turned and came toward him. The animal stopped by Gibson's side, and the rider leaned down from the saddle. With an outstretched hand, he beckoned the cat and 'roo to take a ride with him.

"Gibson," whispered Gracie, breaking the silence, "Let's go. I believe he wants to help us. I'm not sure, but I think this is Czar Peter . . . Peter the Great.

Hesitantly, Gibson and Gracie stepped toward the offered hand and were gently spirited upward and deposited onto the saddle. The steed proceeded to the secret passageway and clopped down the same stairs that Gracie and Gibson had just scampered up. At the bottom of the stairwell, the horse reared up and effortlessly smashed open the door with his front hooves. Then the magnificent stallion calmly marched out into a small deserted courtyard, which is where Ivan caught up with them.

"Hey wait, wait for me! What's going on?" the monkey shouted as he ran into the courtyard, simultaneously hopping, jumping, and spinning in circles. "Are you going to America to ride in an American *Sputnik*? I want to come. Take me with you!" Ivan scampered across the courtyard in hot pursuit of the prancing horse while in the distance a steady chorus of cheers sounded from the crowd gathered in front of the palace.

Gracie, who was sitting on Gibson's back and clutching his ears for dear life, noticed a glowing field of energy starting to build around them. It was, she instinctively realized, residual energy from all the courageous bees that had died coming to her rescue when they thought she was being tortured. Their energy was now combining with that of the bees that had been crushed while opening the bookcase.

Like a shower of molten lava, specks of the energy field descended upon Ivan covering him completely. Several seconds passed, then the little dots of energy faded away into nothingness. Ivan had been replaced by a snake. The drab brown creature slithered on the ground and nipped frantically at the horse's heels. The animal kicked the serpent and tore it into three pieces, sending the chunks sailing through the air. The pieces landed within inches of each other on the cobblestones and immediately merged back into the form of the snake . . . which proceeded to transform itself into a monkey. It was Ivan, sitting on his rump, scratching his head and trying to figure out what had just happened.

Gibson purred, confident he and Gracie would soon be free. Gracie felt secure enough to climb into her rescuer's breast pocket. Her emerald dress billowed out like a festive handkerchief.

In a stately manner, they made their way to the post office, down deserted quiet streets. Everyone, it seemed, had gone off and joined the celebration in front of the palace. As the travelers made a final turn into a wide alleyway the czar's horse suddenly reared back and threw his front hooves high into the air. Peter jerked on the reins, sending Gibson tumbling to the ground. Gracie executed a nimble leap out of Peter's pocket and rushed to Gibson's side. Together, the two hobbled away from the suddenly berserk horse and sought safety.

A loud, thunderous roar halted them in their tracks. The ground began to shake. Cobblestones shook loose and debris filled the air as the ground split apart into a maze of fissures. As Gracie and Gibson watched in disbelief, thousands of skeletons sprang from beneath the street's broken surface.

As the great czar struggled for control over his horse, the sea of skeletons converged around him. As they advanced, they began to regain the same faces and bodies they had enjoyed while alive, complete with the appropriate clothing and accessories their class and profession had dictated. Among them there were merchants, sailors, peasants, doctors, lawyers, servants, boyars, and several animals. Some held knives, pitchforks, and ropes; others displayed books and tools. Just when it appeared the crowd would completely engulf both horse and rider, the steed ceased to struggle and knelt down in a clear display of submission. The czar's hands quivered slightly as he bowed his head deeply to one and all.

With Peter and his horse kneeling before the massed spirits of the dead, the crowd dropped their weapons and returned the gesture. In that moment of supreme mutual respect, a palpable sense of peace flowed through the alleyway and drifted out beyond the streets and squares of the city.

Transfixed by this astonishing tableau, Gracie and Gibson were surprised to discover Aunt Zappa standing beside them.

"Gracie, Gibson, it's time to go. The Time Warp Tube is repaired. The technicians back in the thirty-sixth universe really got cracking when they realized Peter the Great was going to take control of your rescue."

Startled by her beloved ancestor Gracie tried to compose herself. The little 'roo asked, "Please Auntie Zappa, before we go, can you explain something to me? What does all this mean? The people and the czar . . . why are they bowing to each other?"

"I'm not sure, dear. Perhaps, for the moment everyone was willing to forgive what needs to be forgiven."

The ancient 'roo's explanation didn't make much sense to Gibson, although *he* certainly didn't have a better answer. He sensed, however, that everyone in the spectacle had worked together for something really important. Perhaps the beauty and grandeur of St. Petersburg was somehow tied to this one transcendent moment. An interesting theory, to be sure, but not something easily understood by his feline brain. Until recently he'd been just another cat chasing mice through a farmer's field. And now . . . this?

As the friends prepared to take leave, the magnificent scene before their eyes began to disappear. The people,

Peter the Great, the horse, and even the debris from the torn up street vanished. One by one, everything blinked over into an alternate universe. The very real and slightly foreboding bulk of the post office building, now cloaked in shadows, remained behind. A gentle breeze cooled the night air. Silence ruled the city.

As the duo prepared to troop up the plank of the Time Warp Tube that had magically materialized out of nowhere at Auntie Zappa's behest, the ancient 'roo remarked, "By the way, when the Time Warp Tube brings you back here in *your* time, don't get confused. The signs will say you're in Leningrad."

"Why was such a beautiful name for a city changed to Leningrad?" Gracie wondered aloud. "In the thirty-sixth universe, we've always referred to it as St. Petersburg."

"That decision was made by nincompoops," Auntie Zappa explained.

"Ah, yes," Gibson remarked haughtily. "Humans . . . nincompoops--thank goodness I'm a feline."

"A feline who's getting awfully full of himself," Gracie countered. "Come on, let's go."

The 'roo, still attired in her emerald and lace dress, hopped onto the cat's back. They entered the tube to the accompaniment of soothing music and a rainbow of colors. The Time Warp door closed with an ethereal hiss, and less than a millisecond later the transporter vanished. Alone in the alleyway, Auntie Zappa enjoyed a lingering moment of affection for Gracie, and for Gibson, too--the newest addition to her extended family; then, she too disappeared.

Linda Lee Schell

CHAPTER EIGHTEEN

Excerpt from: A COMPLETE HISTORY OF THE UNIVERSES

Chapter 729,513,684

Published by 'Roo University Press

Earth history books claim that the people of St. Petersburg were told their czar suffered from hemorrhoids. The truth is that Peter the Third's reign was brought down by insects.

The bees made a mistake. They believed Peter was harming Gracie. If Peter had hurt Gracie, then their decision to protect the 'roo would have been correct. If Peter had been kinder to his dogs and been more concerned with how he was perceived, the citizenry would not have jumped to conclusions. Peter gave ammunition to his enemies.

The bees had their hearts in the right place. They worked for Gibson and Gracie's freedom even though they expected no direct benefit other than knowing that helping was the right thing to do.

History is full of mistakes, misunderstandings, and unintended consequences. Peter never wanted to be czar of Russia, so perhaps we can say that everything worked out for the best, anyway.

The bees' domicile was found the following morning when Catherine ordered her staff to look for Ivan, Gracie and Gibson. A servant caught Ivan dipping the candle snuffer into honey cascading down the wall of the czar's chamber. Because of the honey's high quality, Catherine moved the bees to special farms in the country.

Now the bees didn't have to travel so far to work. Buttercups, Queen Anne's lace, and every wild flower imaginable stood waiting at the bees' back door. Catherine's decision to protect the four-winged insects proved astute. A large portion of the earth's food supply depends on the honey bee.

No one in St. Petersburg ever saw the czar again. No factual documentation exists, although rumors as to the czar's whereabouts abound. Some say the czar was last seen herding reindeer in Siberia for a portly fellow from the north. Others say a woman and a child resembling Catherine and Paul were spotted on occasion in a town known as Veliky Ustvug.

In that town a frail-looking diminutive man doted on a troika of horses owned by Ded Moroz, known in some parts as Grandfather Frost. Although the strange man was small in stature, the horses obeyed his every command. Some say the man's commands were so forceful, it is as if he had barked orders all his life.

In the end, Catherine's extravagant spending and collecting greatly benefited Russia. Visitors still go to the Russian Versailles to see the artwork Catherine amassed over the years, thereby substantially enhancing the city's coffers. The downside is that people occasionally get lost amongst the many portraits and antiques, and require rescue.

Aside from inconsequential palace rats and mice, and one high-strung peacock, Ivan remained the only animal in permanent palace residence. To the end of his days, Ivan reigned supreme.

The End

53396793R00058

Made in the USA
Charleston, SC
11 March 2016